I0618369

VENICE
Heat

BY

TRESSIE
LOCKWOOD

AMIRA PRESS

Amira Press
Charlotte, NC
www.amirapress.com

Chapter One

Shae stood up and stretched her arms over her head. She'd come to her family home a few days ago after the fiasco with her sister in Juneau, Alaska, but she'd gotten little sleep since then. Aside from the fact that she worried about Shiya, her father's home seemed to be Grand Central Station for everyone in their organization to drop by whenever the mood struck them. Add to this the arguing going late into the night, every muscle in her body ached, and her head pounded despite the pain pills she'd downed an hour ago.

Her bedroom door burst open with nary a knock, and she gritted her teeth in frustration for forgetting to lock it. "Shae, what are you doing here?" Kasen demanded, a scowl marring his face so like their dad's.

Shae glared at him. "Um, I think it's my room, genius."

His nostrils flared, and if possible, his expression grew darker. "Watch your mouth. I'm on E. I haven't had coffee, and Dad and I have been up all night debating what to do about getting someone to replace Shiya. I want to go back out there to Juneau and drag her ass home after I put a bullet in those bears. Dad wants to leave her there."

"For once, I agree with you." Shae stood and grabbed a robe to toss around her figure. Her brother had never respected her or her sisters' right to privacy, and it didn't look like he'd back out of the room with her just in a nightgown. She doubted the man fully recognized her as a woman. How the heck had he ever found a wife? "I want to go get her. They could be hurting her right now, or she could be..."

"Ain't no sense in getting emotional over it," he snapped. "What's important is getting back online. I don't like admitting it, but she knew her stuff. We're wiped out, no addresses, no contacts, no leads. Everything we were working on, except for a possible in Paris, where Sakura is, and one iffy in Taiwan, is gone."

Shae belted the tie on her robe. "So in other words, you don't give a damn about our sister being safe. You just care that you don't know where to find your next kill."

Kasen was on her in a heartbeat, but she blocked the move he made to grab her arm. For her pains, the heel of her palm throbbed, and the ache shot straight up to her elbow. She wouldn't give him the satisfaction of seeing her wince, but stared him down.

"I know you weren't about to grab me. I'm not Sheila or my sister."

His eyes narrowed. "What's that supposed to mean?"

"Read it the way you want."

They glared at each other for a long moment until Shae sighed and turned away. Sometimes she thought her brother was evil and had no heart, but on rare occasions, he showed a softer side. Too bad he reserved that side of him for his son and no one else. Because of his attitude, the first chance she'd gotten, she'd moved out of the family home, so she didn't have to see him often. Kasen lived with his wife, Sheila, and his son, Kasen the third, but he visited their father almost every day when he wasn't out of town on a job.

Rather than stand around and argue senselessly with Kasen, she grabbed a couple of toiletry items and headed to her private bathroom. This time she did lock the door and turned on the shower, glad it and the radio she'd left in there drowned out her brother's shouting voice. She didn't worry he'd break the door down because of his growing anger issues. He wouldn't dare damage anything in their father's house.

After her shower, Shae dressed in a pair of denim short shorts and a halter top. She slipped her feet into flip-flops. Summer was in full force, and all she wanted was to be cool and comfortable.

Later, carrying a cup of coffee and an egg, cheese, and bacon sandwich, she walked down the hall on the first floor of the massive house. The Keiths never did things small. Their house was considered a mansion, with ten bedrooms, three living areas, and one formal and one casual dining room. She had loved the place growing up, but mostly because the halls echoed with her and her sisters' laughter as they teased Kasen. They had never let him hear the end of it the year he favored lime-green pants, which he wanted to wear every day. Their mother had put her foot down, saying he would smell, but even then Kasen didn't have a lot of respect for anyone but their dad. Of course, he would never sass their mother to her face, or Dad would skin him alive, but he'd pack the pants in his backpack and change at a friend's house. Who would have thought he'd land his first girlfriend wearing those hideous things? Shae tried to remember his age at that time and thought it was twelve. Boys were stupid, she concluded, and shook her head.

A wave of sadness overtook her remembering, and she wished, not for the first time, that Shiya and Sakura were home—and safe. After the incident with Shiya, Sakura had called to say she would come back, but their dad forbade it. She needed to concentrate on her job. Shae wished he had allowed it, if only to sit in Shiya's room with Sakura and cry it out together. Well, she would cry, and Sakura would try to cheer her up.

A door overhead opened, and Shae picked up voices. The deep, rumbling one she recognized to be her dad, and the higher one, her mother's old best friend. Shae tightened her jaw. The woman hadn't wasted any time moving in on their dad after Mom died. Shae had managed to avoid spending much time with them together, and she didn't relish seeing the disheveled fresh-out-of-bed look like they were an old married couple. She ducked through a random door as feet appeared on the stairs ahead of her and found herself in her mother's old study.

Shae leaned against the door, looking around. She breathed in deep, and tears wet her eyes. Her mother's scent still lingered after five years. Her father hadn't changed a thing in this room, except he'd hung the portrait he had done of her in here. The smiling face with only the slightest creases around her eyes, along with the long, dark hair reaching past her shoulders, brought tightness to Shae's chest. Her dad had transferred the picture here from the spot above his bed where it had hung for years. Shae knew it was to appease the heifer sharing his bed now, and while she understood it, she didn't like it. She was mature enough to keep her mouth shut about not liking Gladys because Dad deserved happiness just as much as the rest of them.

Having lost her appetite, she crossed the plush wine-red carpet to set her plate on the desk. Then she took a seat behind it and leaned back to stare at the ceiling. Countless times, she had visited her mother in this room and talked to her about boyfriends, falling in love, girlfriends, and even about her sisters. Her mother had never judged her. She'd listened and given advice when Shae asked for it, or was just a shoulder to cry on when Shae needed that too. Their mother had been larger than life, in her opinion, and no one could take her place.

Five years wasn't long enough for the pain of her loss to dull, if it ever would.

After she'd had a good cry, Shae sat up and pulled the folded envelope from her pocket. She smoothed it and pulled the contract from the interior. "Eiji Tanaka," she read, her temporary landlord. She knew from looking it up Eiji was pronounced *ay-jee*, a Japanese name. She liked it and hoped she would like the man's home in Venice, California, which she'd rented for the next few months. The fact that she'd been ordered to go on vacation until Shiya's replacement could be found was probably why Kasen had demanded to know why she still hung around. He could kiss her ass. She would leave when she chose to since she did not answer to him. Kasen had a group of men who were his subordinates, but their dad had made it plain from the beginning, he would not command Shae or her sisters. Kasen seemed to forget the fact regularly.

The door opened, and her dad stuck his head in. "I thought I heard a noise in here. Shae, why are you still here?"

She sighed. "Why is everyone trying to get rid of me?" Her mother's portrait caught her attention again. "Dad, what happened to her?"

He stiffened, and Shae thought she saw anger blaze in his eyes before it disappeared and he forced a smile. Her father and Kasen were so bitter over the shifters. She was too, but the men seemed more intense about it. Maybe it was because they tended toward being old-fashioned, feeling it their duty to protect the women. Her dad must feel like a failure because he couldn't protect her mother.

"You've heard the story a hundred times, Shae," he bit out between his teeth.

"Just once, from you. Kasen drills it into us as if it's the only thing that keeps us girls fighting. I believe in our cause. Those

5

things are dangerous, and I want them all dead the same as you, especially since one of them killed my mother."

Her voice cracked on the last words, and her dad strode farther into the room and shut the door. He moved to lean on the desk and held out a hand for her to put hers in his palm. She ignored the hand and wrapped her arms around his waist, resting her head on his belly. Even at fifty-eight, her dad was solid and toned. She admired that about him. He could hold his own almost as well as the young men under him, maybe better since he knew tricks they hadn't learned yet.

"Your mother was beautiful and perfect," he whispered, his voice coming out only a little shaky. "She didn't deserve what happened to her."

"What was it? What kind of animal?"

He hesitated. "A bear."

Shae let out a small yelp before she could stop it. The two men Shiya was having an affair with were bear shifters. "Shiya."

"Don't," her father ordered, and Shae pulled away.

"But, Dad, she's...They could..."

Her father's demeanor grew cold, and he stood up to walk around the desk. He approached her mother's portrait and stared up at it, hands clenched into fists at his sides. "It happened in Vegas, a routine assignment. He tracked her. I'm sure Kasen told you this?"

She nodded and realized her dad couldn't see her response. Misery closed her throat, but she forced the word out. "Yes."

"He tracked her to her hotel room and tortured her before killing her."

"Surely, someone would have heard—"

"Shae!" The way her father winced, she knew his pain was as raw as her own, and when he turned to face her, she saw the tears glistening in his eyes. Kasen Keith Sr. never cried—*ever*.

She rushed over and hugged him again. "Dad, we have to bring Shiya home. I know if we try now that she thinks we've pulled out of Alaska, we can find her."

"Shae, you will not mention your sister's name to me ever again. After what she did to our entire system, she's dead to me."

Shae gasped. She drew away from him and stared into his face. "You can't mean that."

"She is dead," he growled, "and if you go there, you will be dead to me as well. Have I made myself clear?"

She warred between defying him and doing what he asked. Even at thirty-one, with her sisters one year older and one year younger, she rarely disobeyed her dad. None of them did, not even her brother. This man before her commanded that much respect in the way he carried himself, his strength of mind, and his kindness to all except shifters. Yet, she loved Shiya more than anyone on the planet. For him to tell her not to look for her sister, it broke her heart.

Sure, she could tell her father where to go and brush him off, but he was essentially her boss, and his generous salary paid her bills. Heck, they allowed her to live a life of luxury. None of it meant more to her than Shiya, but she believed in what they were doing. Like her dad and her brother, what the shifter had done to her mother tore her apart. Shiya was a grown woman who had made her choice, and Shae could not chase after her and pretend the shifters weren't dangerous. Cut off from her family and their resources would mean going out into the world not just poor but blind to the monsters that existed. They might be in a terrible bind right now with all their data erased, but she had no doubt they would get it back, even if they had to painstakingly rebuild, following up on every lead one at a time. For now, she needed to do what her dad asked. By no means had she written Shiya off, but she would bide her time for now.

"Okay, I won't go to Juneau."

Her dad smiled and patted her cheek. All the anger drained from his expression. "That's my girl. Now, I want you to pack your things and take a vacation like I told you to. Kasen and I will handle things here while you're gone. Have you chosen somewhere to go yet?"

She sighed and moved away from him. All of a sudden she wanted to be gone, like, yesterday. "Yes, Venice."

"Ah, Italy is nice."

"No, Venice, California."

Her father frowned. "Shae, you know I can arrange for you to go anywhere in the world."

"No, Dad, I got this. I'm going to Venice Beach. As close as it is, I haven't been there, and frankly, since it's practically in our backyard, it's not likely we had any tips of shifters in the area that we haven't already taken care of."

"Hm, you're probably right." He pulled out his wallet. "Do you need any money?"

She laughed despite her dark mood. "Seriously? Dad, I have more than I know what to do with half the time. No, I'm fine. Thanks."

He frowned, seeming disappointed he couldn't help her in that way. She knew he enjoyed giving to his kids. Maybe she should have taken cash to make him feel better. After all, she'd just made him relive the nightmare of finding her mother's body. He really was a good man.

"Okay, sweetheart, have fun, and keep in touch."

"Of course. Thanks, Dad." She walked over and kissed his cheek, then headed up to her room. By tomorrow afternoon, she would be in Venice.

* * * *

Shae spared a quick glance at the dash to check the time. She was almost an hour and a half late for meeting her rental agent and hoped he hadn't left yet. Her last-minute arrangements meant she'd had to settle for a place less extravagant than she'd wanted. While the fantasy of snagging a place over in the Hollywood Hills sounded great, the narrow Venice street she now navigated her car along *so* did not fit the bill. The tiny square bungalow with pea-green walls, brown wood door, and small deck might be cute, but could she stand being surrounded so closely with her neighbors? A Jeep parked out front in the hiccup of a parking space made her breathe a sigh of relief. He hadn't left. She rolled to a stop, threw the car into park, and turned off the engine. While she struggled with two big luggage bags, the front door opened, and a man appeared in the entryway. For a moment, Shae forgot everything except Eiji Tanaka. Could any man be hotter with his cold demeanor reflected in those almost-black eyes? His height took her by surprise, being a good few inches over six feet, if she had to guess, and defined biceps bulging beneath a short-sleeved shirt said the man worked out. Not having a huge build, he wasn't slender as she'd expected either. Eiji wasn't a lot of things—primary being happy.

"You are late," he snapped, and Shae marveled at his accent, heavy as if he'd just stepped off a plane from Tokyo.

"Sorry about that. I hit traffic," she prattled as she righted one of her bags, which had fallen over. "My GPS said two hours, but it lied. I'm Shae Jones." She didn't know what had possessed her to use her mother's maiden name when she reserved the house, other than wanting to step out of her normal life and just have some fun. The Keith name was well-known in the underworld. Shifters avoided it, and the few humans privy to their existence knew they could count on Shae and her family to handle any issues.

Her smile hadn't faltered until she reached the three steps leading onto the porch, and she realized Eiji had no intention of helping her. All her charitable thoughts toward him flew away with her temper. "You must be Ed-jie Tanaka," she simpered and deliberately butchered his name. "Can you give me a hand?"

This time she got a rise. He stirred from his post and walked down the steps with deliberate movements. A whiff of his soap and natural male scent assaulted Shae's nose, and she licked her lips and swallowed, all of a sudden hot for reasons other than the temperature. She wrapped men around her little finger for a living, and not many got her blood pumping without a little effort on their part. Yet this one had her going even while being a jerk.

He nabbed both bags from her hands and raised them as if they were feathers. "It's Eiji—*Ay-Jee!*" he emphasized.

She widened her eyes and just smiled as if that's what she'd said. Any other person would have at least scowled, but Mr. Statue simply snapped the words and disappeared inside the house, leaving her feeling stupid.

"Whatever," she muttered and followed him.

The interior of the place she'd rented was small, but much nicer than its outside. Shiny hardwood floors, contemporary furniture, and simple pictures on the walls of animals such as zebras and lions decorated the square living room. What impressed her was the wide fireplace, accented with a dark wood mantel and the huge flat-screen TV above it, although she didn't have any intention of sitting at home much using either. The kitchen sat directly off the living room, a strip of space designed for efficiency of use. Around the corner from the kitchen, she found a small two-seater eating area and, off from that, the first bedroom. After noting a private bathroom in it, she turned back to Eiji.

"I like your accent. Japan, right? How long have you been in America?"

Something flashed in his eyes, but she couldn't identify the emotion before it disappeared. "Yes, Tokyo. Few months. Is the house acceptable?"

"Wow, you're a great conversationalist." She smiled and leaned against the table, head tilted. "So what's fun to do in this town? Any hot spots you can suggest? Hell, maybe you can show me around."

"I'm sorry." He didn't appear to be. He strode away from her toward the kitchen and stopped at the counter. From his pocket, he pulled out an envelope and set it on the counter. "Your keys and my number if you have a problem."

Well, that was that. She didn't intend to keep chasing after him. There must be hundreds of hot guys in Venice right that second, and she could have a good time with any number of them. Shae had never failed to find the best parties wherever she went. All she needed to do was get out there, and Eiji Tanaka could kiss her ass. She snatched the envelope from the counter and turned on her heel. Her luggage sat nearby, so she bent to grab one to take into the bedroom, leaving the bastard of a landlord where he stood.

Chapter Two

Eiji watched Shae laugh and flirt from where he stood against the wall. He held a drink in his hand, but he hadn't yet taken a sip. Instead he wanted to remain alert because there was no doubt in his mind that the beautiful Shae Jones could not know the man she displayed an indecent amount of her cleavage to was, in fact, a wolf shifter. Eiji had pegged him from the first moment he strolled into the bar. He had paused just inside the door to get a lay of the place, taking in the two wolves buying drinks, one female, one male, the three additional men surrounding their leader at one of the tables, and the very human man at the pool table who eyed Shae with interest from the second she walked in the door.

So she wouldn't turn and see he'd been following her, he'd left the entrance and found an unoccupied spot in a corner—well, almost unoccupied if he managed to ignore the couple making out. This was nothing new to him, since he'd seen plenty in Tokyo, but it wasn't where he liked to spend his free nights either. Earlier, he'd told himself to forget about her and wipe Shae from his mind, but that turned out to be impossible.

When she bent to grab her bag back at his house, his shaft had tightened. He'd scarcely held onto his control with her inches away from him. Her scent had filled his nostrils and sharpened the teeth in his mouth. He felt his wolf rising to the surface, eager to taste her, to touch and take her. From the moment she stepped out of the car, he knew desire he'd never experienced before, a white-hot need to claim a woman. All he could do at the time was fold his arms over his chest, and it had pissed her off. The stance had kept him from tossing her on the hood of her car and slaking his lust with her beautiful mocha body.

He had not chosen to come to America. His life in Tokyo was satisfying in its way, but family matters drove him here, and when it was done, he would leave. Still, he couldn't dismiss her. He'd hesitated at the house, telling himself to leave, but then he had lifted the second bag to take into the room. He'd moved noiselessly so she didn't hear him when he entered the bedroom. She bent over her task of unpacking clothes. Bikini panties landed on the bedspread, and he clamped his teeth together, breathing deep through his nostrils. A human scent, she smelled sweet. *Chikusho!* He had cursed in silence. Shutting his eyes did not erase her from his vision or give him the push needed to leave the house.

After a few moments, he had set the bag down near the door and turned away. Before he could change his mind, he had hurried through the small house to the exit and stepped out to his Jeep. Behind the wheel, he turned over the engine and threw the vehicle into reverse. He would not come back or see her again and ignored the incessant whine from his wolf that this woman, an American of all people, a *human*, was without a doubt *the* one.

That was early afternoon, and yet, here he was, stalking her around Venice, watching her and listening to the delicate tinkle

14

of her laughter. His cock had gone hard and stayed that way, and nothing he could do, no meditation or deep breathing, would calm the beast inside.

He had behaved coldly to her to keep her at a distance. Now she flirted with the alpha of a pack of wolves, and Eiji just kept himself from growling each time the man touched her arm. He focused on the two of them in an attempt to shut out the sounds of all those around and pick up on their conversation.

"What's a sweet thing like you doing out here alone?" the alpha asked while running a fingertip along Shae's arm.

Eiji evaluated his size and strength—a big African American man, at least six foot five, with muscle packed on top of muscle. Despite that, he thought he could take him, but not if his pack jumped into the fight, or even just his second in line along with him. He bided his time.

"Oh please," Shae was saying, a smile spreading over her full lips, "I can take care of myself."

The alpha leaned forward, meeting her gaze with a dangerous one of his own. "Not against me, baby. Don't you know I'm the big bad wolf?"

Shae rolled her eyes and then studied him as if she considered whether he meant it literally. The alpha wiggled his eyebrows and stuck out his tongue in a stupid way that had her laughing. "Is that right?"

"Yeah, that's right."

Eiji's stomach went sour. In the next moment, the man said something else to Shae, and while Eiji heard it, he couldn't understand the meaning. Every now and then his command of English failed him, especially if the person spoke too quickly or if words were used he wasn't familiar with. He uttered a Japanese expletive of his own because Shae appeared excited about whatever it was the man suggested. When a body blocked his vision of her, he glanced up into the face of one of the shifters.

"So, wolf. You see something that interests you over there with my friend and his girl?"

The man standing across from him was also African American, but not so solidly built as his alpha. Eiji guessed he wasn't the second in line either, maybe the third with ambitions for moving up. He sought to intimidate, but it wouldn't work.

"Why don't you shut your mouth?" Eiji suggested.

The man whooped and slapped his hands on the table, laughing. "Why doncha shut you maaff," he teased, squinting his eyes. "I have an idea, why don't I kick your ass?"

Eiji slammed his glass on the table and walked around it, but before he could make a move, Shae stepped between them, a hand on both their chests. Eiji ignored the shockwave that ricocheted throughout his body at her touch, and snarled at his opponent. The man shoved Shae, but Eiji moved in a flash to first keep her on her feet and knock the guy on the floor in the next breath.

Men from the alpha's pack gathered around him, ready to attack, but he noticed none revealed what they truly were. He was pushed to his limits keeping his secret as well, but he waited for one of them to expose it in her presence.

"Whoa, hold on, everybody," Shae interjected. "Darryl, if your boys kick my landlord's ass, I'm going to be out on the street. Call them off, pretty please?" She smiled up at him, holding onto his arm and leaning way too close so that her breasts brushed him. Even across the room, a person could pick up on how she turned the alpha on, but then he seemed to catch on to her words, and he frowned.

"Your landlord?" Darryl snapped. "You know this fool?"

Shae made a sound like sucking her teeth. "Don't be rude. Yes, that's what I said, isn't it? Eiji doesn't mean any harm. He's sweet. Right, Eiji?" She met Eiji's gaze and offered what he now saw as her man-manipulating smile. She'd pronounced his name not as an American would, but with the Kanto dialect. Curiosity about this intriguing woman surfaced in him, and he glanced away.

"You don't need him, Shae," Darryl insisted. "You can come stay with me."

"Boy, please. I just met you, and if you're the type to pick a fight, I'm not sure I want to get to know you better."

"Looks to me like the Asian's the type to let a woman do his fighting for him," another man quipped.

Eiji frowned. "I don't need anyone to fight for me. I will take care of all of you now." He pointed and indicated the group in one. A few of them dropped words he didn't know but suspected were swears. He sensed their tempers ran high, but they held them in check. One command from the alpha, and he would have a lot to deal with. He kicked himself for putting on a show for her benefit like Darryl obviously did. Eiji usually let his actions speak for him and kept his words to a minimum. He did not like risking exposing his kind to humans, and a wolf's temper was enough to manage without provocation.

"Oh, is that so?" the third said and bumped his friend aside to stand face-to-face with Eiji. "The little Asian wants to front like he got swagger."

A couple of the guys laughed, and one called out, "'Little Asian,' Travon? He's taller than you."

This didn't sit right with Travon, and after glaring at his friend, he whipped back to Eiji. The punch came from nowhere, unexpected, fast, and powerful. A human might have seen the blur, but any trained man could swing fast enough to defy the eye to see it. What Eiji knew a human would not see was the strength behind

Travon's fist. If he let it hit him without bracing himself, he would be sent flying backward halfway across the room. He had no intention of taking the punch either way. The analysis of the situation flashed through his mind the instant he noted Travon's jaw tense and the predator's gleam in his wolf's eyes. His fist shot out, and Eiji stepped back with one foot while at the same time raising an open fist to guide the blow away from his face. All around him, people gasped, but he held his defensive stance in case another attack followed.

Shae's mouth formed a small *O*, her eyes wide as she stared at him in silence. The alpha snarled. He curled clawed fingers into his palms, and with some satisfaction, Eiji imagined they'd cut into the man's skin.

"I did not give you permission to attack, Travon," Darryl snapped, his voice harsh and scratchy as if he fought the change.

Eiji shifted his gaze from his enemies back to Shae, but she still watched him, and he knew a bit of relief. She hadn't paid attention to overhear the alpha, so she wouldn't wonder at his control over his men in these modern times. They were being careless and stupid, and he wanted this whole situation to end now.

"I'm not going to have fighting in here," the owner of the bar shouted. "You take that outside before I call the police!"

Eiji stood straighter and looked the shifters over once more before turning toward the door. He made it only a few steps and stopped. He couldn't leave Shae there with them. She would not be safe. He spun around in degrees and met her gaze, then strode back. Inches away from grabbing for her hand, he stopped again. Another thing he couldn't risk at the moment was touching her skin.

He cleared his throat. "May I talk to you for a minute?"

The speculation in her large brown eyes did things to his body he wished the others didn't sense about him. She raised her eyebrows. "Really, Eiji, I think—"

"Please," he emphasized and felt heat flood his face. Snickers erupted around him.

She nodded and walked a few feet away from the alpha and his men. Eiji hitched his shoulders, annoyed that they would hear, but there was no other choice aside from him dragging Shae outside.

"I want you to leave with me," he blurted out for lack of a better way to say what he needed to.

She frowned and put her hands on her hips. "You didn't want to go out with me earlier, and now you're all up in my face?"

More snickers, and Eiji clenched his jaw.

"I don't..." He sighed and cut a glance over to the group. "I don't trust them."

"Hey!" Travon started to approach, but the alpha held him back, amusement in his expression.

Eiji knew he expected Shae to turn him down. The knowledge made him feel even more of a fool. Of course, at their distance, Shae hadn't heard the whispered taunts aimed at him, and the laughter because she wouldn't listen to him. Her attention never left Eiji's face.

He spread his hands out to the side and shrugged. "It's not because...uh, I..." He scratched his head, searching for the right words. "*Hazukashii desu?*"

"What the hell does that mean?" someone across the room asked.

"How the fuck should I know?" someone else answered.

Shae blinked up at him, and an impulse took hold before he thought it through. The next instant, he dragged her into his arms and encircled her waist. He covered her mouth with his and tasted a flavor so sweet he lost track of the men who threatened him and didn't hear the noise of the music vibrating off the walls. All he knew was the feel of Shae's soft lips beneath his own and the way she parted them for him. He heard her murmur of surprise and, if he wasn't imagining things, the tiniest of moans. Seconds later, the alpha wrenched him away, but Shae moved between them once again, this time both her hands pressed to Darryl's chest. When she spoke, she panted.

"Hold on. You don't get to choose who I kiss. You and I just met, so back it up. Now, I've decided. I'm going with him." She indicated Eiji.

Darryl put her aside. "This nobody's got nothing on me, Shae. You can't be serious."

"Oh, I'm serious." She moved beside Eiji, and he resisted dragging her into his arms again. Shae waggled her phone at Darryl. "If you act like you have some sense, I might use the number you gave me tomorrow."

"I don't understand." Eiji stared at her. American women were confusing. Hadn't she just chosen *him*?

She grinned and headed for the door. "Are you coming or what?"

Eiji swept the shifters with his gaze, and Darryl's unhappiness with the outcome of their scuffle radiated off of him. Yet, Eiji could not feel like he'd won. For now, he would spend time with Shae, and maybe he would come to figure her out.

They left the bar and walked along Abbot Kinney Boulevard. Cars zoomed along in both directions, and neither of them said a word for a while. Eiji stuffed his hands in his pockets, head down. Instinctively, he moved around others as they passed going the opposite direction. Every now and then, he glanced at her. Shae's scent filled his nostrils, distracting and alluring. He heard her soft breaths and the beat of her heart as it raced faster than it should have given that they were strolling at an unhurried pace.

At the corner, they stopped and waited for traffic to lighten so they could cross the street. Shae turned to him. "What does *hazukashii desu* mean?"

"How is it you pronounce my language so well?" he countered.

She winked, and something stirred inside him. "I've traveled all over the world."

"Business?"

To his surprise, she hesitated and then shrugged. "I love seeing new places and meeting new people."

His thoughts returned to the alpha, and he frowned. "I see."

She laughed. "No, you don't. So are you going to answer my question or what?"

Now he hesitated and pulled his hands from his pockets to spread his fingers while struggling to come up with the correct word in English. "Maybe it's *em-bass*?"

Her beautiful eyes widened. "Imbecile?"

"I don't know that word."

Amusement brightened her face, drawing him in as if she'd cast a spell. He shoved his hands back into his pockets to keep from touching her.

"Uncomfortable?" he suggested.

"Oh, I got you. Embarrassed!"

"Yes, embarrassed." Heat rose in his face, and he turned to stride across the street. Her shorter legs worked harder to keep up, and realizing his rudeness, he slowed down.

"You didn't want to go out with me, but it wasn't because you were embarrassed to be seen with me?" she said, still working through his weak explanation. She simplified the situation with her words, but she could not know the complications. He didn't enlighten her. "So tell me, Eiji Tanaka, what do you do for a living?"

"I am a policeman."

"Interesting, and I like your accent." He studied her face, and she grinned. "For real. I'm not like those other idiots who teased you. I've always loved the way Japanese people speak, in their own language and in English."

He uttered nothing more than a grunt, which seemed to amuse her further.

"So what are you doing in California? You said you've been here only a few months."

"My cousin." He clenched his hands in his pockets. "She was killed a few months ago. She had lived in America for ten years, seeking fame and fortune in movies."

She touched his arm. "I'm so sorry. I know how hard that can be losing family."

The truth of her understanding was reflected in the sadness in her eyes. He nodded. "Izumi left me her house and some savings. I had to take time to learn how to handle real estate here. Someone advised me to rent the house. You are my first."

"You did good."

He frowned at her treating him as if he were a child learning a new skill, but she laughed. This woman was so carefree and full of life. She seemed to whip about him like a whirlwind, sweeping him along.

"Let's go somewhere to eat," she suggested. "I'm hungry, and I only had a light sandwich earlier. Later, we could walk along the boardwalk, if you want."

He shook his head, and when she appeared disappointed, he explained, "We can eat, but it's after midnight. The curfew is from midnight until five a.m. No access to the boardwalk."

"Well that bites. Okay, food then." She rubbed her flat belly, stirring his desire for something other than *tabemono*. "A sushi place?" They were just passing a Japanese restaurant.

"No, whatever you like," he assured her.

"This place looks good. I'm surprised they're open, but I guess some establishments cater to the late-night tourists. You get the munchies after clubbing sometimes."

She took his hand, and Eiji allowed her to link her fingers with his. He followed her through the doors into the restaurant and found a cafeteria-type setting. People lined up along a glass-encased counter and slid trays along it to indicate to servers what foods they'd like. The atmosphere was familiar to Eiji, which relaxed him considerably. He selected a tray behind Shae and surveyed the offerings of barbecue brisket, Moroccan chicken, mac and cheese, tossed salad, and even rice. All of the dishes were labeled with what they were, but he elected to point out what he wanted instead. At a separate counter, he watched Shae choose two different types of dessert.

"You are too small to eat all of that," he told her.

She simply wriggled her eyebrows at him and chose another dessert for him. At their final destination, a man worked behind a counter making fresh-squeezed lemonade. Shae chose blueberry mint, but he went with a simple coffee, and she shook her head.

He insisted on paying for everything, and they found outside seating at a table with a wide umbrella over it. The restaurant had arranged live plants to line the courtyard, allowing for privacy and separation from the surrounding area. Soft yet adequate lighting allowed them to see without trouble. He hadn't been to this restaurant before and was glad Shae selected it, as long as the food tasted good.

Shae watched him scoop up his Moroccan chicken with rice. "Good?"

"Mmm, very." He forgot about his own meal when her soft lips parting distracted him. When she glanced up, he looked away. To force his mind to acceptable areas, he questioned her about herself. "What do you do?"

The nervous hesitation must have been his imagination because it lasted no more than an instant. "I'm a travel writer. Freelance, mostly, in case you're wondering what publication I work for. I make an okay living."

He considered himself good at his job, pretty decent at reading people, and he knew without a doubt Shae lied to him. He allowed his gaze to glide over her beautiful form while she chattered away between bites of food. Long manicured nails, soft hands did not necessarily indicate she was not a writer. Many women were into caring for their hands and their feet no matter how it might inconvenience their work. Her clothes seemed to be expensive. He was not familiar with Western brands, but he imagined it was not so much different from his own country, as many of his people loved imported American goods—clothing among them. Shae's were high quality, and so was her purse. The diamond earrings and the sterling silver rings on her fingers indicated no shortage of money. Unless, of course, she was a person who would neglect a bill to buy expensive treats. No, this woman didn't strike him as such, and that meant she did more than "okay" at her job. Why did she lie?

"...so with the loss of all the contacts, my boss told me to take a much-needed vacation," she concluded, "and he would call me when he needs me for my next assignment."

He grinned. What she said now rang as true. "Except you are, as you say, freelance, and you don't have a boss."

Her eyes widened, and she stumbled over her words. "You know what I mean. Every editor I've worked with, I call boss."

Not wanting her to feel uncomfortable since he understood a person's need for privacy, he let the matter drop and moved the conversation to other topics. "Do you have sisters or brothers?"

She seized on this. "Yes! Two sisters and one brother. They're all a trip, but I love them. My dad's still around, but my mom passed not too long ago."

He offered his sympathy, and while he wanted to touch her as she had touched him in concern for his loss, he resisted.

"What about you?"

"Brother. My parents, grandparents, and great-grandparents are all here."

"Here in America? That's so cool."

He flushed. "Here, alive. They live in Kurama, not far from Kyoto." He added *Japan* in case she didn't understand his meaning.

They continued to talk until they finished their food. When Shae had sampled both her desserts and finished off one of them, she reached across the table to point at his. "Did you want this?"

He leaned back from his tray. "Please, enjoy."

Eiji relished the view and her moans as she cut small bites from the chocolate pie. She stuck her fork between her lips and slid it out slowly. His cock twitched in his pants, and he clenched his jaw. She must know what she did to him, or she was one of the most sexually alive women he'd ever met. When she finished the dessert, she stuck a delicate tongue out and licked her fork while watching him through lowered lashes.

He sucked in a deep breath and leaned toward her. Dropping his voice low, he asked, "Is this style of eating something all American women do or just you?"

"Wouldn't you like to know?" she teased and stood up. After gathering up her tray, she headed to the trash receptacle and emptied it and then placed it on a counter above the bin. Eiji followed suit, and the two of them left the restaurant.

Once again, on the street, she took his hand and laced her fingers with his. The stirrings of desire in him danced to higher levels. When she noticed him examining their linked hands, she pulled away.

"Oh crap, I'm sorry. I'm used to getting close to a guy really fast—I mean, wait, that totally didn't sound right. Made me sound like a whore."

"Does it have something to do with your work?"

His question earned him a flash of suspicion in her gaze. "No. Not at all."

They walked in silence, saying nothing. Eiji stuffed his hands back into his pockets and decided to watch the people they passed. Even at that time of night, many wore little clothing. Quite a few of the women sported bikini tops rather than blouses.

After some time of discussing inconsequential matters, they ended up back at the house she had rented from him. Eiji waited by her side while she searched inside her purse for the keys. He was about to ask if she'd lost them when the entire bag upended from her hands, and the contents scattered over the porch. He bent to snatch several items up before they rolled off into the dirt.

"Wow, you're fast," she said, sounding impressed. "That was some martial arts stuff you did at the bar, wasn't it?"

He raised his brows at her and didn't answer. A tube of something that might be a type of makeup escaped toward the edge of the porch. He put a foot out to capture it while dumping the rest into her outstretched purse.

"Thanks." Her head tilted to the side brought his attention to the bouncy silkiness to her curls, and he experienced an itch to run his fingers through it. Women with short hair had never appealed to him before.

He stooped to grab the tube and noticed something else, what appeared to be a photograph, facedown. After turning it over, he froze and then took his time straightening.

"What are you looking at, Eiji? Don't tell me I had a naked picture of myself in there." When he glanced at her, she laughed. "I was kidding. What is that?"

She reached for it, and he handed it over. Her gasp told him she hadn't expected it to be what it was.

"Tell me about it," he commanded in a low tone.

Shae eyed him, a curl of annoyance on her lips, but she answered, "It's a picture of my mother after she was killed. I didn't know it was there. I think my stupid brother is trying to pull the mess he pulled on my sister. If he thinks that will work, he don't know me very well."

Eiji frowned. "Your brother?"

"Never mind. Anyway, she was attacked by a bear in Vegas. That's how he left her."

"He?"

Pain filled her eyes, but it disappeared, replaced with anger. "The bear."

"This is right after she was killed? She hadn't been moved?"

"Damn it! Can't you take a hint?" she shouted. "It was my mother, Eiji. Maybe in your culture, it's okay to be so nosey you keep asking questions about how a person's mother passed, but not here. Not with me. Good night!"

She turned and flounced to the door to stab her key through the lock. Eiji leaned out and grabbed her arm to whip her back to face him.

"*Gomennasai.* I'm sorry." He took the picture from her hand. "This is not a bear attack, and it is not in Vegas."

Chapter Three

*A*fter a restless night of sleep, which lasted only a few hours, Shae opened her eyes to sunlight streaming in the bedroom window, directly in her eyes. She'd thought about closing the curtains but had forgotten, her mind so full of what Eiji told her and the implications of what he'd said. Of course, he could be dead wrong.

She dragged herself from bed and took a long, hot shower and then rifled through the clothes she'd brought with her for something appropriate to wear during the heat of the day. Last night, after Eiji left, she'd run into the house to call her father. There'd been no answer. Next, she'd tried Kasen, and Sheila, his wife, had answered his cell.

"Hey, Sheila, I need to speak with Kasen—now, please," she'd demanded.

"Shae, hi to you too. Anything wrong?"

She'd gritted her teeth. "I…well, I don't know. I wanted to speak with my dad, but he's not picking up. That leaves Kasen, and I know it's late, but I also know the man doesn't believe in keeping regular hours, so please put him on."

"He's in the shower. Let me walk in there. Hold on."

Shae picked up sounds of doors opening and closing, and then the unmistakable tapping of water hitting a shower floor. Sheila's muffled voice mixed in, and then Kasen came on. "It's late, Shae."

"Whatever. I want to know why you lied about where Mom died."

"Excuse me?"

She started to tell him about Eiji, but changed her mind. Her brother didn't need to be in her personal life, but then she realized where her thoughts were going. She and Eiji had just enjoyed conversation and dinner. Neither had said anything about taking it further, and while Eiji had opened up some, he still seemed pretty cold to her. That might be his culture, but she'd met Japanese people before. None seemed as closed off as he did. Focusing on the conversation, she'd explained to Kasen the details of what Eiji told her.

"And you assume I'm the one that lied."

"Well, you're the one that told us girls the details. Dad had a hard time talking about it. He still does. We were all out of the country, and you were the one to make arrangements and take care of Dad, who was a mess." She'd started pacing the room. "As a matter of fact, I don't appreciate you stuffing that damn picture in my purse for people to see."

"What people?"

"Jackass!"

When Kasen spoke again, he'd cast his voice low and threatening. She should have known she wouldn't get anything out of him when she made him angry or disrespected him. His ego weighed a ton.

"Don't call me again asking me stupid questions. You're on vacation. Rest up, because as soon as we get even a hint of where to find our next target, I'm putting you on it. Your ass is going to charm the hell out of any and all the shifters I tell you to. If you even imagine betraying the family, I will deal with you."

Shae had shivered despite herself, but she'd demanded, "Who the hell do you think you are, Kasen? I answer to Dad, not you. Or did you forget that?"

He'd laughed. "That's changed as of earlier tonight."

After those chilling words, he'd hung up the phone, and she knew even if she tried, he wouldn't answer anymore of her calls until he was ready. She'd dialed her dad and left messages with no luck. Now, at nine in the morning, she picked up her cell phone to try again. The voicemail came on. She stomped her foot in frustration and threw the phone on the bed. Sometimes if her dad was in a meeting or on assignment—which he frequently was—he didn't answer, and one had to wait until he got free. He always returned her and her sisters' calls. The only thing she could do was wait for him.

Stepping into a pair of booty shorts, she considered calling Darryl, but doubted he'd be awake. He'd been drinking heavily the night before and didn't appear to be the early-to-rise type. She would, without a doubt, call him, though. Dating one man had never been in her makeup, and the determination to remain free of a relationship had increased after her mother died. The devastation her dad suffered after he lost her mom seemed like too much to bear, and it was a strong possibility with their line of work. They'd lost many men and almost lost Kasen once. He bore the scars to prove it. Nope, no falling in love for her. Just fun and sex, nothing serious.

Of course, that meant she could play with Eiji. He looked like he was hung, and the challenge of breaking through the cool exterior might be enjoyable. She picked up her phone and dialed the number he had given her before she drove to Venice from San Diego. Eiji picked up on the first ring, sending a certain warmth spreading through her that she tamed in a heartbeat.

"Hey, I hope I didn't wake you."

"No, is there a problem with the house?"

So they were back to the impersonal stuff? "No, I thought I'd walk along the boardwalk this morning after grabbing some breakfast and wanted company. Are you up for it or too tired from our late night?"

He didn't answer right away, and she waited in silence for him to make the decision. A small, niggling doubt made her question if he was attracted to her, but she dismissed it. Eiji had kissed her, and experience and the hardness that had pressed into her belly told her he liked it.

"I will pick you up," he said and cut the line.

Shae laughed and went back to getting dressed. The man hadn't even waited to arrange the time, so she assumed he would be on his way as soon as he dressed. She wondered where he stayed and determined she'd ask him later. A sense of anticipation stirred in her core, but she didn't suppress it. Nothing wrong with desiring a man, and boy oh boy did she want Eiji. His sexy voice with that heavy accent gave her chills. She'd felt the rigid and defined muscles beneath his shirt when his lips touched hers. Seeing him naked, and soon, meant playing her cards right, which was what she did best. Even if Kasen had been rude and condescending, seducing men was what the Keith sisters did. They lured the shifters into a false sense of security so that they revealed their true natures, and then the backup team came in and took them out. Shae and her sisters never slept with the shifters, of course, but they could bring them to their knees fast. Since she wasn't on the job and just going after a regular man, she could go all out. Eiji would be putty in her hands before the end of the week, maybe sooner. Then she'd see what Darryl was about.

Fifteen minutes later, the doorbell rang, and Shae went to answer it. She opened the door to find Eiji dressed in cargo pants and a long-sleeved shirt. Despite being overdressed, she thought he looked good. "You're going to melt. Don't you have any shorts or T-shirts, or are you ashamed of your legs?"

The glare made her giggle. She dragged him inside, and then, on impulse after she shut the door, she stretched up on tiptoe and kissed his lips. The brush up lasted a heartbeat, and she turned away humming to go put on her sandals. When she returned to the small entrance area, she pretended not to notice he hadn't moved, that it seemed like every muscle in his body had petrified, and he seemed to concentrate on breathing. If she didn't know better, she'd call the man a virgin, but no, he knew a thing or two—at least about kissing.

"Ready?" she asked, amused.

He shoved his hands into his pockets, something he did often, she noticed, and he nodded.

They left the house and walked along the street. "Did you have breakfast already?" she asked. "I'm starving."

He eyed her, but didn't reveal in his expression what he thought of what he saw. The fact annoyed her. She was used to men fawning over her. Not that she expected it or anything.

"You eat a lot for a small woman."

She made a noise with her mouth and waved the comment off. "Please, you haven't seen anything. From the age of nine, when I began training how to kick ass and take names, I've had a big appetite. Maybe it's all the sparring. Whenever I'm in town back home, I spar with my old instructor or any of the other men that work for my dad, to keep my skills honed."

His eyes narrowed. "Why do you push yourself so hard?"

She realized her mistake and could have kicked herself. "My dad's obsessed with keeping his girls safe. He's funny that way."

To her relief, Eiji took this at face value. She figured he put it down to the weirdness of American women, but sometimes in her field of taking out shifters, she ran into trouble. A shifter might catch on before her team swooped in to deal with them. The creature would then try to kill her, and she had to handle her business. Of course, her dad had insisted she and Sakura, her older sister, always have a protector, a man who worked closer to them than the rest, but he might not get there in time, so she had to be prepared. Shiya, her youngest sister, had always worked at home, behind a computer screen, until she took it into her head to get out in the field for the first time. Their dad giving his permission had shocked them all, but they had abided by it. Now Shiya was out in Alaska, in the middle of who knows where, with two polar bear shifters as her lovers. Thinking of it for the millionth time, a niggle of worry ate at Shae,but she shook it off. What captured her attention more than that right now was what Eiji had shared.

"We can go back to Abbot Kinney Boulevard or to the boardwalk," Eiji suggested. "I have eaten at a restaurant there. The food is good."

She turned toward the boardwalk and the beach without commenting, and he shifted directions with her. "Eiji, I guess I was too shocked last night to really question you. How do you know it wasn't a bear attack that killed my mother, and what about that bridge you mentioned?"

He looked away as if he didn't want her to see his face. "I've had experience with animal attacks."

She gasped. "You?"

"No."

When he didn't elaborate, she guessed he'd seen a few cases in his line of work. "And the bridge? I mean, you said yourself you haven't been in America long, and I got the impression this is your first time here."

"Not my first, just not long each time." He stopped walking and faced her, holding out his hand. "Do you have it?"

She'd considered leaving it in the house, but knew she wanted to question him after she hadn't been able to reach her dad. They moved to the side so as not to block anyone passing, and she put the picture in his hand. When he held it up to show her, her stomach knotted, and the usual feelings of loss stirred, but Eiji touched the lower part of her back with such a gentle pressure, she drew comfort from him.

"Look past your mother," he instructed. "See the window? The bridge is there."

"Yes, I know. You showed me all that last night, but—"

"This is what is called Miami-Dade County. You know it?"

She nodded.

He continued. "As I said, this picture was taken in Miami, not in Las Vegas."

"That could be a random bridge. How do you recognize it if you've only been here a few times and not that long?"

"A few years ago, I participated in a video conference with the police in Miami. A drug trafficking ring were operating their business out of Tokyo and smuggling cocaine to Miami. We shared many photographs, which included Asian nationals. A few of the photographs showed this bridge. I spent hours studying them, so I remember it well." He tapped the picture. "This is Miami."

"All this time," Shae muttered as she tucked the photo away. "If it wasn't a bear, what was it?"

She looked up at him as she closed her purse, but Eiji had started walking again. She caught up with him and touched his arm. "Eiji, what did it?"

"I don't know." His gaze had gone cold and his bearing stiff.

"Don't know or won't say!"

"It is not for me to solve this case, but for your policemen. If they did not see the evidence at the crime scene that I quickly saw from a photograph, I don't know how you will get justice."

Her mouth fell open, and she put her hands on her hips. "Are you serious? You're going to go all high and mighty, like we don't know what we're doing over here? This is my mother we're talking about, not some stranger. I know you didn't know her, but she was everything to us. *Everything!*"

Tears flooded Shae's eyes, but she blinked them away. More formed until she couldn't see. She found herself in Eiji's arms, crushed to his chest with his arms like steel bands around her waist.

"*Gomen,*" he whispered in her ear. "I'm sorry. I was wrong."

As far as Shae was concerned, the date was ruined. She dismissed Eiji, telling him she needed to be alone, and she continued down the street toward the boardwalk. Daring a look over her shoulder, she saw him standing there watching her but not following. Even while he had pissed her off and made her cry, which she hated doing in front of others, an urge to go back to him rose inside her. She resisted it, calling him an arrogant dick to keep her feet moving in the opposite direction.

Once she reached the long strip that bordered the ocean, she walked along it, taking in the sights. Early in the day, there weren't as many people crowding the walk, but a few meandered along. A sectioned-off area had been set up as an outdoor gym complete with weights and other exercise equipment. She paused to watch a couple of muscle heads working their biceps and then realized she recognized one. He had been with Darryl the night before, and she remembered thinking he liked to impress his friends too much. He'd shown off coming at Eiji. She suppressed a laugh recalling it. Bet he didn't expect Eiji to deflect his punch with such ease.

Rather than stand around risking Travon noticing her, she moved on. Impulse led her to keep Darryl stewing for a couple days. The city was big enough for her to find plenty of action without him or Eiji.

She found breakfast when her appetite demanded it and spent the day shopping. Later, when the sun went down, she left the house in a mini dress designed to hug her curves and show off more cleavage than was decent. In spiky heels, she slipped into the taxi she had called and instructed the driver to take her to a hot area for clubs. He drove a good five miles at least, and then Shae spotted a place she thought looked interesting.

"Stop here, please."

Traffic forced him to go to the end of the street before he found an opening to let her out. She paid the driver and left the taxi to walk back. Music spilled out onto the street from various spots, and she knew often a club would feature a live band. Lines formed, and people milled along the sidewalks.

"Hey, pretty lady," someone called. From the corner of her eye, the man standing in front of one establishment spoke to her. She raised a brow and eyed him before letting her gaze to the people entering. She didn't spot any women, and the men seemed too excited to get inside.

"Um, yeah, I don't think that's my kind of place," she informed the bouncer.

He gestured for her to come over. "Beautiful women are always wanted, right? You're beautiful. Come on. Have a little fun."

"What the hell." She stepped into the dark interior and was blasted with music. A woman strolled by dressed in a white top that looked like it had been ripped apart to just a strip of material covering her breasts. The shorts—or maybe they were panties from the look of them—didn't cover the lower half of her ass cheeks. Shae scanned the room and discovered quite a few women with their men at the tables. When she stepped forward, a small crowd of people crossed her path, and one of the men holding a bottle of champagne caught her eye. His eyes widened with interest, and he smiled.

"Care to join me and my friends?" He wasn't half bad looking.

"Where are you going?"

"Private party." He winked and jerked his head toward a set of doors to her right. "I'm Jeff, by the way."

"Why not? I'm Shae."

She linked arms with him and joined the procession. The room turned out to be quite large, with several couches. A few dancers were already present, and Jeff's female friends kicked off their shoes and began gyrating with each other and a couple of the men also there. Shae watched Jeff pour her a glass of champagne and thanked him. She took a sip and began swaying her hips as well. An hour or so later, she'd ordered a mojito and a couple shots and had kicked her heels off as well.

Jeff clung as she worked her way around the room, meeting new people, laughing and dancing with a few of the girls. The music blasted nonstop, and she didn't sit down once. When she raised an arm and wiggled her hips while sipping her drink, another girl copied her. Jeff shoveled chocolate truffle bread pudding into his mouth and sidled up behind her. His jerky movements made her wonder if he was drunk or spastic. She didn't know what had happened to the champagne bottle.

Her host's enthusiasm to drag more and more people into his party had the room jam-packed, but when Shae looked out over the crowd, she thought she saw Darryl. She blinked and checked again, and he wasn't there. Well, the place wasn't that big, so if he was around, she would have spotted him. West Los Angeles was a huge city, and she didn't believe she'd stumble onto him so easily miles from the house she'd rented.

At one thirty, Shae stumbled from the bar with Jeff staggering after her. He grabbed her shoulder and bumped into her on his own unsteady feet. "So your place or mine?"

She shifted her shoulders so his hand would fall away. "Thanks, Jeff. It was fun. Maybe I'll see you around again while I'm here."

He stuck his bottom lip out, looking like an idiot. She was even less inclined to encourage the man. "Aw, don't be that way. I thought we had chemistry. Didn't you feel it? We could finish the night with a different kind of fun."

"Yeah, no." She rolled her eyes. "Good night."

Before she could walk away, he grabbed her arm and squeezed. "I bought all your drinks."

She let her gaze drop from his face to his hand. "*Thanks.*"

"You owe me something."

"I will give you three seconds."

From nowhere, Eiji stood between them with a hand jacking up Jeff by the collar. Shae squeaked and darted forward to tug on his arm.

"Whoa, Eiji, dial it down. What are you doing here?"

He spared her a glance and glared at Jeff. "He will not take no for an answer. I will show him."

"I can take care of myself, but thanks. Let him go."

Jeff flopped around hanging from Eiji's hold, and even though Eiji pissed her off for acting like her protector, she had to admire his strength. Jeff was no little man. He had Eiji by an inch or two and probably by a good fifty pounds. Still Eiji raised him to his toes. The muscles in her landlord's biceps bulged with the effort and strained against the material of his T-shirt. *He's wearing a T-shirt?* Somehow she believed it was in her honor.

A small crowd had gathered around him, and Jeff's drunken friends shouted comments. Shae peered up and down the street for the cops. They would be there soon, no doubt. She tugged at Eiji's arm. "Let him go before you get arrested."

As if those were the magic words, Eiji let go and stepped back. Jeff almost crumpled to the ground until two of his friends stepped up to catch him beneath both arms. "Your loss," he mumbled to Shae, and they dragged him off.

Shae glared at Eiji and spun away toward the street. She spotted a taxi and stepped out to wave him down. He glided on past, the backseat already occupied. She swore and waved for another, but it seemed everyone and his brother had left the clubs at the same time. She started walking, and Eiji caught up.

"I have my car. I will take you home."

She rolled her eyes at him.

"You will not find a taxi now."

"Fine! Take me home."

She walked beside him in silence, and when she couldn't bear to take another step, they turned a corner and came upon the Jeep. A sigh of relief escaped her as she slipped into the passenger seat and removed her heels. With the top open, the warm night air blew her short curls around her head and sobered her up some. She rubbed her feet, moaning. Across from her, Eiji alternated between clenching his fist and rubbing a hand over his taut thigh. She tried not to notice, but couldn't help wondering what was on his mind.

A short while later, he drew up in front of the house, and she got out barefoot. "Thanks."

"Shae."

Despite herself, she liked how he pronounced her name. It was all kinds of wrong, but she didn't care. "What?"

"I'm sorry. I didn't mean to…"

"Okay, okay. Good night." She turned to go, but he caught her hand and gave a small tug that spun her around to face him.

"I want to see you again."

"No."

He kept her from leaving again. His gaze traveled her length, and she knew he saw how her nipples had hardened behind the thin dress, especially since she'd skipped wearing a bra. She licked her lips, trying to pull herself together. The effect Eiji had on her was the exact opposite to the one Jeff had evoked. Tempted to invite him in, she stood there fighting with her resolve. When she opened her mouth to answer, he dropped her hand and faced the car.

"What, you changed your mind?" Sarcasm dripped from her words, but he didn't answer. He stared off down the street and seemed to sniff the air. Shae frowned at him. "Is someone out there?"

"No one important."

She tried peering through the darkness, but saw nothing. Streetlights stood a couple houses down the block, but no one lurked in the dim illumination that she could see. Maybe he had better night vision than she had.

He focused on her.

She spun on her heel and headed up the steps. "I'll call you."

Eiji didn't try to stop her again as she headed inside the house, and soon the sound of his engine turning over reached her room as she prepared for bed. Tonight, she didn't want to just fall into bed with him, but the next time, all bets were off. He would be hers.

Chapter Four

Shae unfurled her blanket and laid it out carefully on the sand. She tossed her bag down and kicked the flip-flops she'd worn from her feet. Crouching, she dug through her bag for sunblock and began rubbing some on her arms. Aware Eiji watched her, she pretended not to notice and continued with her task.

"Your skin is brown like chocolate," he commented.

Shae laughed. He was no poet, that was for sure, but then she had to give the man a break, sure he had no need to practice being eloquent in her tongue. "Yeah, it is."

"You don't need to tan."

"This isn't tanning lotion, man. It's sunblock. Like you said, my skin is brown, and I love the tone of it. This little beauty"—she waved the tube—"is to keep it that way, so I'm not all crunchy by the time my vacation is over. Mind getting my back?"

She undid the tie on her beach cover-up and watched his gaze sharpen. The pink bikini had been a good choice being that it set off the undertones of her skin. From the look in Eiji's eyes, he agreed. She let the material fall to the ground and turned, giving him a view of how little of her ass the bottoms covered.

"If you could help me down here too, that would be great. Thanks." She pointed to her ass and thighs.

Eiji appeared behind her, less than an inch away, as if he'd teleported there. He squeezed her shoulders and growled in her ear. "You play a dangerous game, Shae."

"I don't know what you mean." She blinked up at him over her shoulder.

He nabbed the tube from her fingers and began squeezing cream into his palm. Shae suppressed a laugh. She knew how to play a man, to give him a little to keep him yipping at her heels in hope of getting more, and then keeping him at a distance so she never had to sleep with him. Of course, that wasn't the plan with Eiji. She fully intended to enjoy this sexy Asian to the hilt, but for now, she would not confirm it with him.

After he had done her bidding, Shae waited until he, too, rubbed sunblock on his skin and was in the middle of it to tease him. "See you later, slowpoke. I'm going for a swim and to have some fun." She pointed at a random group of men heading down the sand toward the water. "Oh, that group looks like they're having a blast."

She took off running, laughing at the grunt of annoyance behind her. If she thought she would get away or that Eiji would let her play with other men, she was sadly mistaken. He caught up to her in a heartbeat and swept her off her feet. Shae kicked and squealed, splashing water with her feet.

"Let go, let go," she said, laughing. "You better not throw me in, Eiji, or else."

The crazy man had the nerve to toss her in the air as if she weighed nothing, and her scream became real. She came down fast, but he caught her to his chest with ease. Soon they were engulfed in the water, and Eiji's teasing turned gentle. He held her hand, and when they went so far out that the waves knocked her about, he stood as a buffer between her and the ocean. She drifted into his arms and pressed light fingertips to his shoulders. His warm skin, with rivulets of water dripping off of it, brought a burning desire to her entire being. The fact that, even in the chilly water, he grew thick and hard, his dick unyielding against her belly, did nothing to cool her down.

She forgot to play the game, getting lost in his eyes. Sometimes, she thought they were paler than usual and knew it wasn't a typical trait for Asians. Maybe he was mixed. She didn't care. His eyes were beautiful.

A cry nearby caught both of their attention. She turned to look and spotted a man drunk as hell trying toss young kids in the surf. "One more, one more," he slurred to a boy of about ten. "Don't be a wuss."

Shae scanned the shore for a lifeguard, but Eiji was already moving past her to approach the fool. "Eiji, what are you doing?"

He didn't answer, but tapped the man on the shoulder. "Get out of the water."

Shae slapped a hand over her mouth to cut off a snicker. Talk about straight to the point.

"Who you think you are, pal, the police?" the man demanded. His face and shoulders reddened as if he were ready to explode. Eiji seemed unperturbed.

"Leave the water now, or I will make you," Eiji repeated.

Something of her landlord's seriousness and his ability to carry out his threat appeared to get through to the guy. As fast as he'd blushed, he paled, but still he tried putting up a front before the kids, who were all laughing at him by now.

"Why don't you go ahead and make me, tough guy?"

The challenge had scarcely left the dude's lips. Eiji did some kind of move on him too fast for Shae to track, and he had the guy over his shoulder, wading to the shore.

Damn. I so need to get with this man!

Shae followed. "Eiji, you shouldn't be interfering with other people. You know they crazy out here." Her halfhearted advice fell on deaf ears.

A lifeguard hurried up as Eiji dumped his burden into the sand. "I think he's drunk."

The lifeguard nodded and thanked him. Eiji took Shae's hand and led her back down the beach toward their stuff. She shook her head at him as they walked. "Always on the job or what?"

He eyed her. "Would it be better to wait until he hurt one of the children?"

"Touché." She bit her lip and ran a hand up and down his arm. "Wanna call it a day and go back to my place?"

Eiji's gaze dropped to her cleavage. "*Hai.*"

* * * *

Shae had had her share of lovers, so she wasn't new to sex by any means, and yet, she hadn't been with an Asian man before. Not that she thought it made any difference. Eiji was hot as hell with his thick black hair and his eyes almost as dark. His solid build, delicious hard muscle, and his tall frame worked together to light a flame of burning desire, more than she remembered experiencing before. Of course it could just be that—lust—and nothing more. His accent helped, too, and the way he had looked into her eyes earlier that night and taken her hand in his. Five foot seven was not tall, but she'd always felt big because of her personality and confidence. Eiji made her feel brand new and small. Damn, how she liked that, the flutter in her belly, the fast pace of her breath.

By the time they arrived back at the house, they were both dry from the hot California sun. Shae's need hadn't lessened in the least, and from the way Eiji followed swiftly on her heels into the house, neither had his. They dropped their things in the living room, and she continued on through to her bedroom.

She stopped at the entrance and faced him. "We're doing this, right?"

"We are." He reached up and touched a lock of her hair, pushing it back from her forehead. She captured his hand and held it, then walked backward into her room until she reached the bed. All the while, she kept her eyes on him. He followed, his gaze never wavering from her as if he were a predator.

Still looking at him, she kicked off a flip-flop, and the other followed. An animal, that's what she'd been thinking of. Eiji sometimes put her in mind of those shifters. Sure, she agreed that they should always be put down for the danger they posed, but she had never denied how hot they all were. *Mm, yeah. Eiji is like that, but better.*

He didn't have the cocky self-assurance like all the shape-shifters she'd met. Not that Eiji was shy. She knew better than that. He wasn't clumsy or less coordinated than the rest. Tilting her head to the side a little, she considered him. He breathed in deep, that big chest expanding and making her mouth water. When he walked, the steps he took made no sound at all. *Yes, that's it. He's like a sexy ninja who doesn't need to show off about it.* She almost laughed out loud at her thoughts.

She undid the buttons on her sundress and pulled it over her head. Eiji's eyes almost glowed at seeing her bikini again. Shae worked hard on her body, so she knew it looked pretty good. She waited for the inevitable compliment, but it never came. In fact, his facial expression never changed from its usual calm indifference.

"Eiji?"

His fingertips skimmed over her bare arms and across her belly. A thumb brushed her thigh and then stopped just short of her mound. "*Anata ha eroppoi.*"

"Rope?"

"You are sexy."

Then she saw it, the way he blew out breaths through his nostrils, the rapid rise and fall of his chest, the intensity in his eyes, and the tension in his shoulders. Eiji liked what he saw, all right, and it took all the self-control he could muster not to jump her, but he didn't have to resist.

She tugged at the button on his pants. "Come on, baby. Let me see what you have for me." A tremor passed through her. Although she felt she could work with any man to bring them both to mutual pleasure, she was like many women. She liked big cocks. The bulge in Eiji's pants drew her hands, and she stroked him through the material. A shudder of need weakened her knees, and she sagged against his chest. *Nice!*

He undid the button on his own and dragged his zipper down. Next went his swimming shorts, and her mouth watered at the revelation of his lean hips and the smattering of dark hair that came into view. Eiji's cock had to be eight inches, if not an inch more, and the girth let her know she'd have to stretch wide to get her lips around it. Precome beaded the tip, and she sank to her knees to lick it. Eiji gasped and pulled her away. At first she thought she'd insulted him, but when he lifted her up and placed her on the bed, she knew Eiji wanted to pleasure her first. He shed her of her bikini within seconds, along with the rest of his clothing.

While she lay on her back, he rested a knee on the bed below her and parted her thighs. He stroked the sensitive skin at the back of her legs, and the inner flesh. "I do not have as much control as I would like."

48

His voice rumbled deeper than it had been previously, and the timbre raised goose bumps on her arms. Eiji bent to kiss the back of her knee. When he stuck his tongue out to sample the skin, she moaned.

"It would be better that I walk away," he whispered and kissed her clit. She shook from head to toe. He pushed back the folds of her softness. "But you are so wet, and you smell so good."

"E-Eiji."

He licked her cream, and she scratched at the sheets. Damn, he went straight for the kill and made her so weak, she wanted to give him everything. She raised her legs higher and held them up with a hand behind each knee. Eiji licked her from the base of her pussy to the top, and then he clamped down on her bud to suck hard. A wave of pleasure rocked her body, making her scream his name again. An orgasm built inside her, but she wasn't the type to just lie still and let a man do all the work. She wriggled away from him and crawled up the bed. Eiji let out a growl that sounded like a real animal and followed. Just before he pounced, she feinted to one side and jumped on him. A move she'd learned in training had him on his back and her on top of him. She pushed his hands out to the sides of his head and straddled his hips.

Eiji's eyes blazed. "You are sneaky." His cock twitched beneath her ass.

"I don't know what you mean." She lowered her butt onto his shaft and ground into him. He groaned. The next instant, she thumped onto her back, and he lay above her. He claimed her lips, his tongue stabbing savagely into her mouth. She kissed him with as much hunger and raised her hips. Eiji slashed a leg over hers, pinning her to the mattress. She broke the kiss. "No fair using your strength against me."

At his look of triumph, she gave him a wicked grin. The

moment he paused to wonder what she was up to, his hold on her hands loosened, and she broke free to reach between them. Stroking his cock and teasing the head with her thumb, she took control of the man two times her size. Shae flipped him off of her and grabbed hold of his cock again. She licked the head, tasting the salty come. A shudder passed over Eiji while he stared down at her. She took him deeper between her lips and moaned against his shaft. He drew in a sharp breath.

"Mm, I know you like that, baby, don't you?" She ran her tongue along the thick length and curled it around the tip. He said something in his language she didn't understand, but she could guess.

"Your mouth," he murmured between clenched teeth, and he reached out to stroke her cheek. He let her pump him with her hand and work him with her mouth for a long while, but when she ran a thumb over his balls and noted they began to tighten toward his release, he pushed her roughly away.

Shae sat up to protest, but Eiji was off the bed in a heartbeat. He hauled her into his arms and wrapped her legs around his hips. She scarcely had a chance to draw in a breath before he plunged his dick deep inside her pussy. A hand knotted in her hair behind her head, and an arm like a steel band encircled her waist. Eiji thrust hard and fast and began pounding in and out of her at lightning speed. She screamed, but he drove her head down and claimed her mouth. The invasion with his hot tongue robbed her of speech. He took her with a violence that demanded submission. Her core muscles spasmed, ripples of an orgasm shattering her ability to do anything other than feel. How had she thought she could get the best of him? She couldn't. Not in a million years.

He stood on legs set apart, strong and steady. He didn't waver even a little as he drove his big cock into her wet pussy. She whimpered and held on, digging her nails into his shoulders. He thrust and thrust again, and then he slammed in and held still.

"*Chikusho!*" He jerked out of her, but held her close to his chest. "I'm sorry."

"Don't be. It was good." She climbed down from his arms to go to the bathroom to find something to clean them both up. They'd been too eager, and she knew better. She kept condoms in her purse for situations like this. He'd pulled out, but not before he'd come a little. When she returned to the bedroom, she found him pacing, running hands through his hair. His brows slashed low over his eyes, and his set jaw told her he was pissed at himself. In the short time she'd known him, she hadn't seen him so worked up.

At her step, he spun around to face her, and she gaped at the stiffness between his legs. The man wanted more after all that. Not that she was complaining. She walked over to the dresser and searched her purse for a condom. He moved behind her and rested hands on her shoulders. For a minute, she thought she saw something odd in his eyes, but his lids lowered over them. He dropped his hands to her breasts and kneaded them, rolling her nipples between a forefinger and a thumb. She moaned, pushing her ass into his thigh. He explored farther, running a palm down her belly and between her legs. A gentle squeeze had her keening for more. Her juices had already begun to flow again.

"Give it to me," he commanded, and she handed over the condom.

Eiji tore into it, and she enjoyed the show of watching him roll the protection down his thick member. She licked her lips, both anticipating being full of him and a little nervous. When he was done, he turned her to face him, the mirror at her back. He raised her with ease and thumped her ass on the dresser. Her pulse raced as the fire he'd exhibited before rose yet again. He thrust her knees up until she hooked her heels on the edge of the dresser.

"I can have it again. Yes?" His words might have been a question, but they sounded more like a demand, and the force of his dominance sent chills racing each other over her skin.

"Yes. Please take me, Eiji."

Her use of his name seemed to set him off the same way his use of hers did for her. He spread her legs wider and fitted his big body between them. With an expert movement, he parted her pussy lips and drove deep into her channel. She cried out in ecstasy. Again and again, he drove inside, stretching her walls and filling her up. She worked her fingers in his hair and sought out his lips. They kissed, moaning into each other's mouths. Shae's nipples ached as they scraped against his bare chest, so stiff with her rising desire. Ripples of pleasure rolled through her body, and she gyrated her hips in time with his thrusts.

For long minutes, they fucked, and she clung to him, loving every time he pounded into her pussy. He was so rough, like he held little restraint over his lust. Before he came, he pulled out, and she would have complained, but he raised her into his arms again. With a set stance, he ground into her snatch and took all of her weight, but even that wasn't enough for the two of them. Eiji set her on her feet and pushed against her back. She spread her legs and leaned over, holding herself up with her hands flat on the floor. Eiji stepped behind her and bent his knees to give himself easier access to her ass, and then he lunged deep again. His fingers dug into her hips, and the slap of their bodies together resounded in the room. Shae echoed it with her cries of ecstasy. Eiji's hold firm, he pushed fast and hard into her. His low growls sent chills up and down her spine. Her breasts jiggled with each impact, and she reached between her legs to stroke her clit. A hiss escaped Eiji, and he rested a hand on her back, but didn't slow down for an instant. When her orgasm began to build, she tweaked her clit faster, keeping the steady rhythm.

"I-I'm going to come," she panted.

"*Hai.*" He spoke some other words in his native tongue, which made her wonder if he'd forgotten how to speak English in his excitement. Shae let the words tumble over her and gave herself to the pleasure of her climax. Seconds after she came, Eiji made a small sound at the back of his throat and found his release as well.

He straightened, then pulled free from her. She struggled over to the bed, gasping for breath. The *slap* of the condom coming off his cock preceded the ripping noise of another packet being opened. Shae had scarcely raised a knee to climb onto the bed before Eiji was there behind her, an arm around her waist. He hoisted her to the top and laid her on her side. He moved in to spoon her from behind and crossed her arms over her chest. She didn't think his cock was still hard, but the stiff member found its way to her treasure, ready to go. Her drenched nether lips gave him easy access to glide inside her. She whimpered. No man had taken her with such relentless abandon. From her experience, no man *had* such stamina or could stay hard so long.

Eiji went beyond every lover she'd ever had. He held her in a tight grip, making it impossible for her to move away. Still from behind, he took her nonstop. She could do nothing other than enjoy the feel of his possession of her body. She shut her eyes and laid her head on his shoulder. He nuzzled the side of her neck, and she thought she felt his teeth graze her skin. Even this turned her on, and she surrendered to her man.

"Eiji," she whispered, "I don't want you to stop. I can't get enough."

"Neither can I," he assured her. "I won't stop until day."

He kept his word. Exhausted and sore, Shae saw the beginnings of daylight pouring into her window before Eiji pulled out of her for the last time, and she drifted off into a very satisfied and much-needed sleep.

Chapter Five

Shae stumbled to the bathroom holding her sore pussy with one palm as if it would fall off if she didn't. After days of lying with Eiji in her bed, she'd sent him home. When he called the next day, she hadn't answered. The endless sex was too much. She had to wonder when the man had last had it. Every muscle in her entire body hurt like hell, and before their marathon, she would have said she was in top form, the best physical condition anyone could be. Eiji's sexual desire was both raw and wild. Sure, it felt out of this world, but for the first time, she thought she couldn't handle a man. He was too much, way out of her league.

She stood in front of the bathroom mirror looking at herself. The dark circles around her eyes, the swollen lips, the tangled hair were not just the aftermath of a satisfied woman, but a woman who needed rest and nourishment. When was the last time she'd eaten? At the thought, her stomach stirred with hunger. She showered first and drew on clothes with sluggish movements before walking into the kitchen to find food. Coffee brewing and bacon frying in the pan, she remembered her cell phone and returned to the bedroom to grab it. The light blinking indicated she had messages, and she pressed the button to unlock the phone. A tingle of fear and excitement stirred to see Eiji had sent a text. She had a voicemail from Darryl, which drew curiosity, and her dad had returned her call. She hadn't heard any of these messages come because she'd been out so deep.

Rather than check her dad's message, she called him first and got his voicemail. She swore and backtracked to the message.

"Hello, Shae, sweetheart, I'm sorry we keep missing each other. I think I might have someone to bring our systems back online. Just not sure he can be trusted yet. Also, handling a potential shifter in New York. Your brother is off to London. I'll share the details when I'm back on the West Coast. I love you. Rest and enjoy yourself. That's an order. Good-bye."

"Damn it!" She'd burned the bacon. After that disaster, she waited until she'd cooked everything and finished eating before she contemplated her next call. She could forget everybody and go shopping. She could hunt up something fun to do until the night scene came alive, which she loved more than anything.

"Or I can admit I'm avoiding Eiji," she murmured into the empty room. Turned out vacation wasn't all it was cracked up to be, at least not alone. She was used to going to exotic or domestic places that were nice, but she wasn't alone. Her posse came along, especially her protector, who was a good friend, one she'd had a no-strings-attached sexual affair with a few years ago. They still slept together when her well went dry. Yet, right now, she both wanted Eiji, and he scared her. She didn't allow things or people to scare her long. She decided she'd give her and Eiji a break. Getting too wrapped up in him could not be allowed to happen.

After a day of shopping and then lounging on the beach in a bikini, she started back to her room thinking she'd give her protector a call and ask him to join her out here. They could have a little fun without any obligations. As she strolled up to her place, smiling and a little excited about her decision, she paused at the shadow that had just flitted behind a building to her right. The sun dropping low in the sky didn't provide much light, but as she stared, she didn't catch sight of anyone. Maybe her imagination played tricks on her. She continued on only to stop once again at the foot of her stairs.

"Darryl, what are you doing here?" She eyed the man from head to toe, noting he still looked fine as hell with chiseled muscle and confidence in spades. He had folded his arms over his chest and leaned with negligence against the banister. None of his boys seemed to be around.

"I got tired of waiting for you, so I came to get you."

"Oh, is that right?" She chuckled, somewhat annoyed and pleased too. She'd written off checking him out, but him showing up was kind of nice. She liked men to come chasing after her. "I've been busy."

To her surprise, his expression went from bored to angry in a heartbeat. "I know, and you made the wrong choice."

"Excuse me? Maybe you should just go. I told you I would call you if I was interested. Now I'm not. So——"

She moved to push past him, but he grabbed her arm to stop her. The bite in his hold set off her warning bells, and she drew in a deep breath, ready to put his ass on the ground. He'd grabbed the wrong woman.

"Come on, baby girl," he whispered. "You know how bad I wanted to get to know you, and you didn't even give a brother a chance."

All her anger ebbed away. She stared into his face, shocked at how open he seemed, even vulnerable. Black men, from her experience, didn't do that often, which made her curious. His thumb caressed the skin at her elbow.

"I guess I could do something tonight," she offered. "I heard about this spot where the dancing is hot, and the drinks are stronger. Wanna check it out with me?"

He grinned and pulled her close. "I would prefer it just be me and you, naked and getting our freak on."

She resisted rolling her eyes and pulled from his hold. "You a little fast, aren't you? I want to dance." She unlocked her door. "If that doesn't work for you…"

"Fine, but you're going to be mine in the end anyway." He smacked her ass, which always pissed her off, but she ground her teeth and didn't complain about it—*this* time.

"Pick me up at—"

"I'll be here at nine. Be ready for me." He stepped off the porch as he slid dark sunglasses into place on his face. She just kept herself from smacking them off and changing her mind yet again. That vulnerability bullshit was just that, and she couldn't believe she'd fallen for it. But anyway, her protector would take a bit to get there when she called him, so she needed tonight, and going to the club alone wasn't as much fun. Darryl would do for now. Tonight, though, she planned to knock him off his high horse and show him how she felt about men telling her how it was going to be.

That night, she wore a red halter mini dress with three openings in the front leading down to her navel. The sides were square cutouts from her breasts to low on her hips, and the ruched details on her thighs and at the back showed off her curves and pronounced her ass. She slipped her feet into high-heeled slingbacks and wore three-tiered gold metal earrings.

At nine fifteen, when Darryl hadn't shown up, she left the house intending to go out to the main street and flag down a taxi. At the corner, a sleek black convertible almost ran her down in the narrow side street, and she flipped the bird at the driver. The car rolled to a stop in front of her, and she swore. Darryl stepped out of the dark interior with music blasting.

"I said I was picking you up," he snapped.

"Yeah, at nine. I wasn't waiting on you." She started to walk around the car to keep going, but once again, he grabbed her arm. She couldn't help comparing him to Eiji. Even at his coldest, Eiji had been polite and considerate.

"Let's go."

She glared at Darryl. "No, I think I'm going to go alone."

"Come on, Shae. Don't be like that, baby girl. We're going to have a good time. Look, I'm sorry, okay? One of my boys was acting stupid today, and I had to set him straight. He made me late. If you want, I can call him up and prove to you it wasn't my fault."

She sighed. It was never their fault. "Darryl—"

"Please?" He did that low-toned whispering thing he'd done earlier, and despite herself, she felt tingly over it. She must be getting weak to fall for little dumb tricks like that. Darryl touched his forehead to hers, as if he was trying to create a closeness between them, like they were already a couple and understood each other. She'd done that kind of thing a million times and recognized it.

"Last chance," she warned him.

He saw her into the car and even held the door while she settled into the low seat. Then he shut it and jogged around to his side. Shae watched his athletic form, the easy grace he displayed as he folded into the driver side and threw the car into gear. In seconds they roared down the road, narrowly missing pedestrians and other vehicles on the street. Shae breathed a sigh of relief when they pulled up to the club and the valet took the offered keys from Darryl. Her ears needed a break from the blaring speakers in the trunk, but she knew it wouldn't be much better where they were going. How Darryl wasn't deaf she didn't know.

Her date must have had pull in this city because he gave the bouncer at the door a nod, and they bypassed the line. A smile spread over Shae's lips, and she clasped Darryl's arm. "Okay, you're doing better so far."

He grinned down at her. "See? I got this, and you're going to be all mine before the night's over."

She laughed, already knowing she would go home alone.

They squeezed into a spot at the bar, and Darryl ordered them drinks. She selected a mojito to start off with, and he had a beer. Darryl pulled her after him toward a spot by the wall, and she settled in front of him to sway her hips to the music. Although early, the place creaked with wall-to-wall people. Several sets of male eyes drifted over Shae's figure in appreciation, but they frowned when they spotted Darryl.

"Damn, you are killing me with that dress, girl," he shouted into her ear.

"Thanks." She turned her back on him and took a sip of her drink.

He moved up close and danced with her. Song after song, they swayed to the music, and she lost herself in the beat and in a couple more drinks. Darryl kept a possessive palm at her waist or splayed over her stomach. No one dared come close, but she didn't mind.

"It's getting late. Let me take you home, and we can continue this," he suggested.

"No, I don't think so," she shouted back and wiggled for the first time from his hold. "I'm going to the ladies' room."

She weaved through the crowd, leaving him standing there. When she was closed off in the small room with other women standing at the sinks and peering in the mirror, she checked her purse for her cell phone. There were no messages. Maybe she should let Darryl take her to get something to eat. They could talk a bit more and get to know each other. He wouldn't like it that she opted for food instead of sex, but he could get over it.

An hour later, they found a table at a nearby spot. She crossed her legs beneath the table and smiled at Darryl. "You sure you don't mind coming here, right?"

"No, I don't mind." The tightness around his mouth said otherwise, but he hadn't pushed. She gave him credit. He picked up the after-midnight menu and perused it. "So what do you want to eat? I'll pay for it."

"Thanks. I think I can handle mine." She studied his handsome face, the brown, intense eyes, and the strong jawline. His nostrils flared a little, and he blew out a strong breath. She had the impression of patience about to snap, but somehow felt it had nothing to do with her spreading her legs. Then again, maybe it did. Most guys were led around by their dicks. Darryl had made it plain he wanted her for himself. His declaration made it seem like he wanted something more long term, though, which was why she hadn't told him to go fuck himself. He wasn't all bad.

By the time Shae tucked into her steak and mixed vegetables, conversation between them flowed. "So what do you do?" she asked him.

He shrugged. She noted how rare he liked his meat and cringed. "A little this and that."

A hustler, she surmised.

"I have a big family to look out for. Everybody turns to me to make sure they eat, but I can handle it. Been doing it for a long time."

"I hear that." She settled back in her seat and saw how his gaze dropped to her breasts. He made no effort of hiding where his attention had wandered. "I have a pretty big family, but while we're close, it's not on any one of us to take care of the rest."

"I know."

She raised an eyebrow at him.

"I mean, I know everybody has family, and yours is probably not like mine," he rushed to say.

Shae stared at him. What he'd said sounded like a cover, but why should it? She was being paranoid and pushed the suspicion out of her head.

"So are you native to Los Angeles?"

He rolled his shoulders as if in relief and continued to eat. "No, I'm from Chicago originally. We came here looking to spread out a little. I had a bit of trouble at the start, but I've made it mine."

Shae laughed. "Man, your ego is huge, isn't it?"

He splayed his hands, and she shook her head. Conversation continued to flow between them without a hitch, and when they finished eating, Shae paid for her part of the check, and they left. She had been glad to see Darryl kept his head while drinking, so he had no problem driving her back to her place. When he pulled up to her rental, she thanked him and hopped out to jog up the steps. The slam of the door behind her made her turn.

"I said thanks, Darryl. I'll call you tomorrow. Definitely, this time."

His hands were shoved deep into his pockets as he ascended the stairs, his face hidden in the shadows of the night. He didn't speak.

Shae took a defensive stance. "I know you're not going to be stupid."

"I'm a lot of things, baby, but stupid's not one of them."

"Why do I hear a threat in there?"

He advanced on her. She held up a hand to ward him off, but in a move that took her unaware by its sheer speed, he had her against the door with his big body grinding against hers. He breathed deep at her neck as if he took in her essence. One hand held her wrist in a viselike grip at her side, and the other might as well be useless the way he pinned her in place.

"You've got three seconds to get the fuck off me," she growled.

"Come on, you didn't tell that to the stupid Asian dude."

"Why do you keep referring to him like that? He has a name."

"You like him!"

"That's none of your business, and as a matter of fact, I think we're done." She brought her knee up to plant in his balls, but he blocked the move and slammed her into the door. She cried out, splitting pain going through the back of her head. Now all kinds of alarm bells went off. She'd been able to take out any regular man for years, but no tricks of her trade dislodged Darryl. Shae stiffened and swallowed. She looked up into his face, struggling to see him clearly. Beyond his head, the moon shone brightly in the sky, but it probably only served to illuminate her face. In the darkness, he chuckled, and goose bumps broke out on her flesh. Her dad's voice rang out in her head the times he'd led the instruction classes she and her sisters had attended. *"Don't get so full of yourself and your ability that you can't scream for help. Do it. It just might save your life."*

She took in a deep breath, but Darryl anticipated her plan. He wrapped a hand around her throat and squeezed just enough to cut off her breath. Panic blinded Shae, and she kicked him hard in the leg. He winced and stumbled. She thought she had a chance when his hold weakened, but the moment she made a move, she regretted it with another slam. He laughed.

"You ain't figured it out, yet, have you, Shae?"

Ashamed, she found herself pleading. "Darryl, don't do this. You can have any woman you want."

"You got that right." He leaned in and ran his nose along her throat. Revulsion turned her stomach, and tears filled her eyes. *Eiji, help me.* Darryl laughed again as if he could hear her silent plea, and she hated her weakness. Shifters had cornered her plenty of times in the past, but she'd held her own until her protector could arrive. This was a dumb-ass man with an ego too big to accept her rejection, and she'd been foolish to trust in her abilities so much. She'd thought he was no threat. At that point, all she could do was pray someone would happen along or he made a mistake that would give her an opening. All she needed was to get space between them.

Darryl rattled the keys she'd left in the lock and turned the doorknob, still holding her by the throat. He shoved the door wide and backed her into the house. With the lights off, Shae couldn't see a thing, but she brought up a layout of the place in her mind, searching for a weapon, a lamp she could crack over his head.

He kicked the door closed, and the lock sliding into place sounded like a death toll. She struggled to swallow, and again she brought up her knee. This time she made connection. The second he doubled over, she brought her knee up into his chin and tried her best to knock his nose into his brain. Darryl turned his head, so the blow glanced off the side. Then he moved fast, before she could straighten to slam a fist into his knee, and sent her leg shooting down toward the floor. She twisted her ankle and snapped the heel off her shoe. Nausea forced her to swallow over and over, and when her stomach settled a bit, she gritted her teeth against the pain, refusing to give him the satisfaction.

Sakura, her oldest sister, would never find herself in this situation, and if Kasen found out, she would never hear the end of it. When she thought of the lack of actual sympathy she'd receive from her family, she had to admit they weren't anywhere near natural. She'd always viewed them all as being close, but how could they be when she couldn't imagine anyone feeling anything other than disgust. Tears of frustration ran down her cheeks.

"Aw, don't cry, baby girl," Darryl whispered. "You're going to thank me for this later on. Well, after you pay for kneeing me in the nuts."

If he called her by that pet name once more, she might lose it. "You're sick if you think any woman would thank you for this. I'm going to get loose, and I'm going to kill you."

In the dimly lit room, she saw him throw back his head and shout with laughter. "Oh man, you're going to be fun with that attitude. I'm going to teach you how to show your man respect."

She spat in his face, and the crack across her cheek brought the taste of blood to her tongue. She swallowed the pain and threw a punch to his solar plexus. Not even flinching, Darryl spun her around and grabbed her by the neck to force her to her knees. Her ankle throbbed anew, making her light-headed and bringing bile to her throat.

With her good leg, she kicked out and connected with his calf. His feet slipped out from beneath him, but it brought his huge bulk down on top of her, flattening them both on the floor. All air left Shae's lungs, and she gasped to take a breath. Darryl pinned her hands together above her head, but he made no moves to touch her body. If only he would turn on a light. The closest switch lay near the table where she could grab the glass vase, but he didn't make a move that way either. He seemed to enjoy the cover of darkness.

"What do you want from me?"

"To make you mine," he answered without pause. "Haven't I been telling you that from the start?"

An idea occurred to her. "You could have been more patient.

You're hot, baby. You know I would have let you in my bed soon enough." She tried pushing her ass up toward him and not throwing up in disgust at the same time. His dick swelled behind her, and she coughed to cover the gag.

"Mmm," Darryl moaned and kissed her neck. "Oh, we're going to fuck, all right. As much as I want it. But first I have to make you ready to be mine."

"I don't know what you mean."

He leaned up, and before she could make a move, he flipped her to her back and lay flat on top of her again. The cry that escaped her couldn't be held in. Darryl brought another to her lips when he ripped the top of her dress open. The swell of her breasts was in full view, the nipples just covered by the torn material. Now he was getting to what she'd known he wanted all along, yet she didn't get the way he expressed himself.

He leaned down to kiss her, but she turned her head. He wrenched it back to face him, but he didn't attempt to claim her lips again. "I'm going to devour you." Moonlight glinted through a gap in the curtains, perfect timing to illuminate his sharpened teeth.

Slow, tormented understanding began to dawn. Her eyes widened until they hurt.

"You thought I didn't know who you were, didn't you? I knew you right away. I picked you out that first night at the club. What did you say your name was? Shae Jones. Naw, that's not you. You're Shae Keith. One of *the* Keiths—shifter hunters. Shifter *killers!*"

Devastation descended on Shae, making her lose all the strength in her body. She could no longer fool herself into thinking this was some kind of mistake or that she could get the better of Darryl the minute she got a toehold. He was not human, which was the very reason none of her blows did any damage. The reason she and her sisters were ever able to kick a shifter's ass was because they knew what was coming. They knew their target, and they made damn sure they were never backed into a corner. Period. All this time, Shae had thought Darryl was human, so she'd taken him for granted. Now, she was in trouble, and she couldn't expect help because she hadn't had the chance to phone her protector to invite him to Venice.

"So you're going to kill me," she said, searching her mind for a way out despite the reality of her situation.

"Kill you?" He patted her head, and Shae struggled to knock his hand away. "No, I'm not going to kill you. I keep telling you what I'm going to do. You don't listen. That's why I need to teach you." Darryl ran his hand down her side, for the first time caressing her body. He stopped at her thigh and gave it a squeeze before jerking her dress upward. She fought as hard as she could against his hold to no avail. By accident, she managed to bump a knee into his balls again, and he cracked her head against the floor. Spots danced in her vision.

He reached for the hem of her dress, but then he paused for the second time. She thought he tormented her on purpose, to drive her fear higher. If she didn't get loose, he would rape her. That couldn't happen. *Please...*

"I'm not going to kill you." Darryl's voice had gone very deep and scratchy, and she knew from experience he'd begun to let the beast inside him take control. He dropped his voice even lower. She had to fight to understand everything he said. "Do you know most shifters in this world can't make new ones like themselves? You're either born with the gene or not, and even that doesn't guarantee your other side will come out. But my kind...Can you guess what kind of shifter I am, Shae?"

She pressed her lips together refusing to answer. He took hold of one of her hands and forced it to his mouth. He dragged her fingertip over the long, sharp canines, and her mind raced. Any number of shifters formed sharp teeth like that. Even Shiya's boyfriends' canine teeth could grow out like Darryl's. Was he a polar bear?

"Can't guess?" Darryl taunted. "I'll give you a hint."

A growl started in his throat that brought her damn close to wetting herself. She shut her eyes, unable to prevent the quake that shook her from head to toe. Killing wolf shifters was hard because they were pack animals, and their abilities bordered on magic. During her training, she had learned about them but never personally come across one, and now she knew that the men she'd called Darryl's boys were also werewolves. She and her family had never known the wolves existed so close to home, and here she lay unprotected. Panic rising until it cramped her stomach, she reviewed his words in her mind. *Do you know that most shifters in this world can't make new ones like themselves?* No, he couldn't mean to do what she thought.

"I can see you," Darryl teased. "You figured it out."

"You can't—"

"I can do what I want!" His words sounded like those of a spoiled child, but his anger scared her more. He released one of her hands to grasp her throat and forced her head to turn, exposing her neck. Shae fought with new resolve, but he didn't give an inch. All she did was wear herself out, and her throat dried at the realization that he intended to bite her.

"Darryl, you don't want a Keith as a shifter, and it doesn't matter anyway. My family will only kill me. We don't take prisoners."

He laughed. "You're a dumb bitch."

She frowned. "Fuck you!"

Instead of the blow she expected, he leaned down and licked her cheek. She gagged openly this time, and he growled. "First,

I'm going to make you a wolf. That's necessary. You know why? Because I can't make you my true mate until you're a wolf. Oh, I heard about your sister Shiya and how she took two bear shifters on. That's what gave me the idea. They're idiots, though, and I'm smarter. See, they might be mated to her and will follow her wherever she goes, but she's a free agent. She can decide today or tomorrow to leave them."

"But you want to control me."

He tapped her jawline with a finger from the hand holding her around the throat. "Bingo. As alpha, I can control my pack, and once you're a part of my pack, I can control you to a certain extent. You could still decide to betray me. But as my mate…"

His wicked grin stole her ability to breathe, and he shook her a little as if to remind her to take a breath. She pulled in a bit of air. Fresh tears burned her eyes, and a knot formed in her throat.

"As my mate, you will be devoted to me. In fact, you will live and breathe devotion to me. You will betray your own family for me. Got it, Shae? You, baby girl, are going to be all mine. First I change you, and then I mate you. Then together *we* rule the Keiths. It's a perfect plan."

Hot tears rolled down the side of her face, into her hair. "Darryl, think about—"

"No more talking." His teeth sank into the base of her throat, and he covered her mouth with a heavy hand just as she screamed. Blackness danced around the edge of her vision as the pain blossomed beyond reason. He sank his bite deeper, ripping cruelly into her flesh. A moan escaped him, but she thought it had more to do with the triumph of beginning his plan than an enjoyment of the taste of her blood. He didn't drink, but let the thick liquid roll down her neck, onto the carpet. Soft whimpers echoed in the room, and it took a while for her to realize she made the noise. After some time—she might have passed out—

the pressure on top of her disappeared. She didn't see him get up, but heard him moving about the house.

A light clicked on, and the toilet flushed. The sink water came on, and Darryl hummed. All throughout Shae's body, her muscles spasmed, but she had no strength to rise from the floor or to call out. The spot where Darryl bit her burned, and the poison he had set loose in her blood seemed to spread fast, down her neck, across her chest, and farther.

The bastard returned and stooped over her. He pulled her eyelid back, alerting her to the fact that her eyes were shut. She'd had no idea. He continued to hum and moved his hand to her neck. A thumb brushed over the wound, forcing a squeak from her. She could muster no more than that.

"I guess I'll give you a break and put you to bed." He lifted her without effort and carried her to the bedroom. The light he turned on made her wince, and the throbbing headache she'd developed intensified. Standing over her, he played with the material of her torn dress. "This is all mine now, but don't worry. I'm not ready to fuck you yet. See, the way I like it, a human woman couldn't take it. I'd break you. When you're fully wolf, then we'll fuck like bunnies."

He laughed at his own joke, and she turned her head. From the curse, she figured he didn't like her attitude.

"You'll think I'm funny soon enough."

"Because you'll force me to?"

His heavy steps led to the door and out to the kitchen. Soon she heard the front door open and close. Seconds after, an engine roared to life, and Darryl was gone. Shae lay where she was, uncovered, with the light beaming down on her. The fever and delirium started sometime later, and she didn't know if it was day or night, if she would live or die.

Chapter Six

*F*or the first time in what must be days, Shae opened her eyes, and the light didn't blind her. Not completely anyway. Every muscle still pulsed with pain, and the migraine hadn't receded. She'd found no ability to rise from the bed today, so she lay there unmoving, existing. Her cell phone had gone off countless times, and the ringing noise had hurt so bad, she'd wept. Sleep escaped her, but then she thought she must have passed out a few times too because sometimes daylight streamed through the window and often moonlight.

She longed to call her dad for help, but she hesitated. She'd spoken the truth to Darryl as far as she knew it. Keiths did not spare shifters no matter who they were. She believed it was a matter of time before her dad ordered his men back into Juneau to kill Shiya's boyfriends, so it was for certain he would do the same to her. Even if she never turned, she was infected and could not be allowed to live.

Nausea assailed her, driving her to make an effort to leave the bed. Today, she made it onto the floor on her hands and knees. She collapsed and then managed a shuffle to the bathroom. Head hanging over the toilet bowl, she dry heaved for a good hour and then passed out on the cold tile floor.

In the bedroom, her cell rang, and she whimpered, covering her ears. Something nearby made a *shooshing* noise, and then a flowery scent like a fist rammed up her nose. She screamed. The hacking came back. "No, no, I can't. Please, I can't do it again."

Darkness descended.

"Shae? Shae, open your eyes. *Okiru.* Wake up."

She blinked at Eiji. Concern creased his brows and darkened his eyes. He raised her in his arms and carried her into the room to lay her on the bed. She breathed deep and yelped in fear, rolling away from him.

"It's okay. I'm not going to hurt you." He reached a hand out to her, but she scooted farther down the bed toward the opposite side from where he stood. She inhaled again and smelled it, that scent so familiar and yet terrifying. Scanning the room, she couldn't identify what it was. Eiji stirred into her line of sight, but he made no move to approach her. "Do you know who I am?"

She licked her dry lips.

"Shae, do you know my name?"

"Eiji." Her voice came out hoarse, and she remembered crying out in pain so long, but no one had heard or come to help. Not even Eiji. Although she'd sobbed nonstop, it surprised her when water clouded her vision. She scrubbed a hand over her eyes and glared at him. "Why are you here now? Why couldn't you come when I needed you?"

"*Gomen.* I would give anything for this not to have happened to you."

She blinked. Did he know? Of course he didn't. He probably thought that bastard had attacked and raped her, nothing more. The next minute he'd be telling her they needed to call the police and report Darryl, but she knew help from the authorities—help from *anyone*—was now beyond her.

"He should have killed me." She hung her head, and Eiji appeared by her side in a heartbeat. He drew her onto his lap, but this time she couldn't mistake the scent. She screamed and scratched his arm. Unlike Darryl, Eiji didn't force her to stay in his embrace. He let her find her footing and back away until she bumped the wall. The exit from her bedroom lay on the other side, behind him. "You're...you're..."

"I'm not one of them," Eiji said, his tone low.

"Liar! I can smell it. I can smell everything, and it hurts like a mother!" She pushed the back of her hand to her nose. "That scented thing in the bathroom is killing me. I smell you, Eiji. You're a shifter. You smell just like Darryl!"

His broad shoulders slumped as he stood before her, but he made no attempt to close the space between them. "I am a wolf shifter, but I'm not one of his pack. I am what you call a rogue wolf, like my cousin Izumi was before me."

"Your cousin?" She frowned.

"The one I told you about, the one who died, the reason I came to America."

The *shooshing*, and she whimpered. Eiji patted the air in a gesture for her to stay where she was. He turned toward the bathroom, and she had the thought to escape, but all the strength she'd used to stand abandoned her. The most she could do at that moment was sink to the floor and try to stay awake.

Something cracked in the bathroom as if Eiji had ripped the air freshener from the wall. She knew it had been screwed into place. He came back with it in his hand and carried it from the room. How could he bear the smell? A few days ago, before this mess happened to her, she'd loved it. Now her stomach turned, and her nostrils burned.

In the kitchen, water came on, followed by a few clicks and bangs. The refrigerator door opened and closed. She capitulated to gravity. The *thud* from landing face-first on the floor sounded dull, but she passed out nonetheless, and when she opened her eyes again, she lay on the bed. Eiji sat on the side, removing her clothes.

"Get off me," she screamed and hit at his hands. He caught her wrists in a grip she couldn't escape from. The humiliation of meeting a second man she couldn't beat was too much. She kicked out, aiming for his nuts.

Eiji swiveled his hips to the left with the ease he'd used that night he blocked a punch. She hated him.

"Stop fighting me, Shae. You are still ill. If I don't help you, there's still a chance you will die."

"It's better if I do."

He glared at her and shoved her down with her hands at her sides. For some reason, with him so close yet not touching, she felt even more vulnerable than she had with Darryl. Eiji, with his quiet self-assurance, his air of being there but being far away at the same time, pissed her off and drew her to him.

"I don't want this."

"You will live, and you will be wolf."

"No!"

Without ceremony, he stripped the last of her clothing from her and left her naked. She peeked into his face as he turned to toss the dirty garments on the floor. Not even a hint of desire cracked his visage. That should reassure her, but it irritated instead. She checked his crotch. Fucker didn't have a hard-on either. *What does it matter? I'm losing my sanity.*

Eiji left the room, and she began to shiver. At first she thought tossing a sheet over her, covering the goose bumps that had popped out along her arms and legs, would do it, but then her teeth chattered, and she gasped for breath. Just as panic set in a roaring fire in her belly so strong she had no energy to scream,

Eiji reappeared and put a cup of some foul-smelling black liquid to her lips. She managed to get a floppy hand lifted.

"Get that away. It stinks."

"Drink it."

"No!"

He put an arm around her shoulders and raised her toward him. The sheet slipped, and her bare breast flattened against his bicep. "Drink it, or I will force it into you."

She darted her gaze to his eyes, expecting anger, but found no vehemence. He jiggled the cup, waiting, and she nodded. The crap tasted like liquid dirt. She choked, but Eiji kept the cup to her lips until she'd swallowed it all. To her surprise, when the last bit went down, the fire in her belly eased, and the shaking subsided enough for sleep. She shut her eyes and forgot everything until the next time she woke up.

This time she sat in bed with a nightgown on, a blanket pulled up to her shoulders. Eiji brought in breakfast of a boiled egg and dry toast. She tried not to wrinkle her nose at it.

"Tell me about your kind," she demanded. "Are there a lot where you come from? In Japan?"

"No."

"You told me you have a brother and parents and grandparents."

His movements were precise as he arranged food on her plate and stirred her tea. After tapping the spoon on the side of the teacup once, he set it aside and turned the cup with both hands, but she didn't know why because it wasn't like there was a handle she needed to grab. She reached out to try her ability to pick it up, but it wobbled, and he helped her take a sip.

"And great-grandparents," he corrected her as if no time had passed. "*Okaasan* is wolf."

"Oka…" she repeated. "Your mom?"

He nodded.

"And?"

"All of the women."

That shocked Shae into silence. She sat there watching him, knowing she smelled it strong on him, but since she had no training to tell her why she smelled the wolf on Eiji, and if all the others smelled that way even if they weren't, she didn't know what to make of it. On the edge of her mind, she still felt panic. She wanted to give in to more tears and scream and rage at him for not protecting her, as if that was his fault. There was something else too, something at this point she was too scared to broach with Eiji. At least in her semi-reasonable right mind, she didn't believe he intended to hurt her.

Rather than approach the biggest fear niggling at her mind, she asked him, "Do you know who I am too?"

"Too?"

"Also."

He appeared to think about it. "Shae Jones."

So Eiji might have been hiding what he was, but he didn't know she was a Keith. Maybe—and it was a slim chance—he hadn't heard of her family at all. She didn't want to tell him. He might have lost a few of those women in his line who were shifters and held a grudge. She'd told him she wanted to die, but she hadn't meant it—at least not now. But as each hour passed, she felt the virus spread. At some point—she wondered if it were only at the full moon—she would change, and from that point on, she would be a wolf shifter, no longer human. Maybe she wasn't considered human now.

A teardrop rolled down her cheek, and Eiji leaned over to brush it away with his thumb. He moved closer and kissed her lips. Shaking and lost, she clung to him, allowing him to share his warmth and his energy.

"I won't always be on my back," she whispered when he moved away.

"I know."

He ended up feeding her as if she were a baby and letting her sleep the afternoon away. In the evening, she went through another rough patch where Eiji force-fed her more of the mud drink. All the time, Shae strained her ears to pick up sounds outside the house, wondering when Darryl would come back. She wanted to warn Eiji and tell him to go away for his own safety, but to be left alone seemed more than she could bear. She knew it was selfish, but when he held her in his arms at her weakest points, she let him.

One night Eiji took her outside on the porch and sat in a chair with her on his lap. The night air cooled her fevered skin, and she didn't complain that she was strong enough to sit up by herself.

The entire time she'd kept her eyes shut from exhaustion, but now she opened them and peered into the night. "I still can't see anymore than I could before."

"You will later."

Shadows shifted, but whether it was a figment of her imagination, she couldn't tell. "We shouldn't be out here."

"They won't come yet."

She jumped at his words, and Eiji's arms tightened around her. "T-Tell me about your family again. Why are only the women wolves, and does that mean you can't change?"

He didn't say anything at first. She wasn't sure if he considered whether he wanted to go on protecting his secret from her or if he weighed whether he should force her to talk about Darryl.

"Many years ago, during the Edo period in my country, wolves were viewed as being evil. Because of this, they were hunted and killed until they were near extinction. Some believe this is why my ancestors sought to become shifters—to hide among humans."

Shae twisted around to look at him. "Are you serious? You think you're originally from animals?"

"Am I wrong to say you are taught here that humans evolved from monkeys?"

"Please, don't even get me started with a religious debate. Anyway, that doesn't explain why only the women become shifters in your family."

"You may not know, but there are many types of shifters in the world."

She didn't bother correcting him in his assumption.

"Families carry the shifter gene, but not all members become shifters. Some are limited to a few or skip generations. Wolf shifters do not follow all the rules of the others."

She clenched her hands into fists on her lap. "So I've learned."

"More or fewer rules can surface among families. Mine is not all women, just mostly women. Over generations, a male can arise."

"You?"

He pressed his lips together. She wished she knew more, but he was so reticent, and she was scared to learn something she never wanted to know. Shae sat back and thought of his situation to avoid thinking about her own.

"Is your brother jealous of you for being something he's not?"

Eiji started and looked down at her.

"Am I wrong? Sorry. I didn't mean to offend you."

"You have not."

"Why didn't your mom or great-grandmother just make all the men like her? She could have bitten them all." She might have spoken the words with a calm tone, but the moment the words left her lips, a pain started in her neck. The spot Darryl bit throbbed, and she shivered with cold and fear. Eiji encircled her in his arms and drew her back to his strong chest. She nuzzled her face in his neck. What would she do when the sickness passed? Where would she go? She reached up to touch the mark, but Eiji caught her fingers and pulled them away. He'd bandaged the spot, and she hadn't seen it.

"The weight of being what I am is heavy, an honor for only those who are born this way," he advised her and frowned. "This man is dishonorable for turning you."

"This man. You mean Darryl. You can tell it was him?"

"I know his scent from the first night."

She licked her lips and swallowed. "Eiji, what's going to happen to me?"

"You will live."

"I mean beyond that. Am I going to…We don't know a lot about the wolves, funny enough. They run in packs and are considered more dangerous than the others." He looked at her, and she spun away to face the street. "I know a thing or two about shifters, but just in case you're wondering, I did not want this! Darryl attacked me, and the first chance I get, I'm going to kill him."

"You won't."

"I will! How are you going to tell me?"

He sighed. "You will come with me to Japan."

"Excuse me?" She wriggled in his arms, and after a bit of struggle, he let her go. She stumbled, and he guided her to the chair he'd occupied while he stood up. She panted like she'd just run a marathon. When would it end?

Eiji stood in front of her, arms folded over a powerful chest, legs apart and firm. "You will become my mate and come with me to Japan to live there from now on."

Shae took her time looking him over from foot to head and down again. She let a slow grin spread over her face, and the bigger it became, the tighter his eyebrows gathered over his dark eyes. His full lips had thinned into a straight line, and his nostrils couldn't flare any more than they had. Still, the sex appeal rolled off him in tidal waves. Rather than let the anger at his words make the top of her head explode, she laughed. The humor felt good after days of pain and terror.

"Boyfriend, you have bumped your everlasting head," she said when the mirth died away. "I know a little about your culture, so I get some of how you think, but let me tell you here and now, I am not the one. When I'm all well, I'm getting out of here. I don't know if I'll go back home, but wherever I decide to go,*I*,and nobody else, will be the one making the call. So, no, I'm not going to be your mate, as you call it. Not now, not ever."

She pushed past him and stormed into the house, or as much as she could in her condition. Having made it all the way to the kitchen, she paused at the refrigerator and tried opening the door. Her stomach stirred, and all the various scents of food behind the barrier called to be eaten. "Damn it, this door's stuck. That idiot probably spilled something and didn't clean it up."

Eiji's arm came around her waist. She'd heard him seconds before he touched her, the bastard. He reached past her with his other arm and easily opened the refrigerator door. Everything inside, from the milk to bottles of juice to several bowls of cut-up vegetables and fruit, was neatly arranged. She should have known better.

"Sit down." He pushed her into a chair, and helpless to resist, she did as he asked. Eiji pulled out a few bowls, and she rubbed her stomach, her eyes widening as she watched him prepare a meal. Precise hand movements, expert slicing techniques, and ease of creating a colorful cuisine took her breath away. He glanced up from adding a mound of sticky rice to a bowl in front of her and smiled. The tension he'd displayed outside disappeared, and he almost looked like a boy. "You're hungry more often."

She moaned. "Yeah, I can't stop eating. If I gain weight, I'm taping my mouth shut."

"Don't worry. Your metabolism is changing and your body structure along with it. That requires a lot of energy. You must feed your body as much as it needs. I will prepare it."

She offered her grudging thanks. "You really shouldn't be here."

He glanced at her.

"What's that look for?" She grabbed the bowl from his hand, and a tingle of pleasure zipped through her being when their fingers touched. She ignored it and scooped up a huge bite of rice without adding the soup he'd made earlier. If she didn't get a least a little in her tummy, she might pass out.

"The only reason *he* is not here is because he knows I am here," Eiji announced.

She chuckled. "Why, because you're that badass?"

He frowned as if he didn't understand the meaning of the word. "He does not care about you."

"That's obvious. Not that I give a damn." She ate all of her plain rice and then held out her bowl. Eiji scooped up more, and this time she added soup to the top. All of his various choices of food were in different small bowls, and he ate using chopsticks. Knowing she would have snapped them in half in a rage, Shae had chosen a soupspoon for everything. "I get the feeling you're going somewhere with this conversation."

He set his chopsticks together and laid them to the side of one of his bowls. "Darryl"—the name was spoken with such derision, she was surprised he didn't spit on the floor after speaking it—"would be here or have one of his men here with you to be sure you don't die during the turning, but he knows I am here to care for you. Why waste one of his people's time, or worse, get into a fight that might leave you dead? Instead, he allows me to do it. When you are fully turned, he will come back. When that happens, he will mark you and force you to be his true mate. No other man will be allowed to touch you."

Shae blinked. "His true mate. Wait, I think he said something like that. Well he can forget it. Nobody's forcing me to do anything. I told you I'm not going with you, and it's for damn sure I'm not going with him. Now that I know what he is, he won't get the drop on me. You think I'm joking, but I'm dead serious. His ass is mine in the worst way."

Eiji retrieved his chopsticks. "You cannot be a rogue wolf, Shae. You must be marked and mated."

"What kind of double standard bullshit is that?"

He didn't say a word, but Shae vowed to show both him and Darryl. They could kiss her ass if they thought she would limit herself to one man or the other. She'd been calling the shots in her life for years, and just because this mess happened didn't mean it would change. Besides, sometimes during the day she felt fine and thought it had all been some kind of big joke. After all, there were people in the world who were psycho and thought they were shifters but weren't. Shae and her family had come across those kinds too. Either way, Darryl was getting his, and while she owed Eiji a lot for looking after her, that's where it ended. In a little while, she would be fine, and then it was on and poppin'.

Chapter Seven

Shae sat curled up on the side of the bed, watching Eiji sleep. For the first time in days, normal levels of strength coursed through her body, but now she had a new issue. Eiji had worn only pajama bottoms to bed. His chest bare, he stretched out on his back, and she hadn't been able to take her eyes off the sexy contours of his flesh for the last hour. Leaning close, she'd breathed in his scent, manly and somehow wild. She'd stuck out her tongue to have a taste, and he'd stirred. With supreme effort, she had forced herself to move away, to look but not touch.

Her sexual desires had always run high, even as a human. While she liked to conclude the coming change was a mistake, a figment of Darryl's and Eiji's imaginations, the fact was, today, her lust went beyond all reason. Even the way Eiji's chest rose and fell at a slow and steady pace tantalized her. His scent filled her nostrils, and when she had tasted his skin, her pussy had gushed with wetness. She glanced down and wasn't surprised to see her nipples rigid behind the thin material of her nightgown. They ached with a need to feel Eiji's fingers or lips on them. She had a feeling if she pulled her gown up and touched her clit, she'd scream with a great orgasm. This was not natural. That she knew.

"Eiji," she whispered, and he stirred once again, but he didn't open his eyes.

She curled her fingers into her palms to keep from ripping at his pants to get a look at his cock. Remembering how rough he'd been when they had sex made her mouth water and her breath raspy as it left her body. What if he said no? She skimmed fingertips over his flat nipples and groaned low in her throat. Surely, he wouldn't do that to her.

"Damn it, Eiji, it's eating me alive."

She grabbed the waistband of his pajama bottoms and dragged it lower. His beautiful cock came into view, semi hard. While she stared, control ebbing from her being, it grew tighter, longer, thicker. She darted her gaze to his face. He looked back at her with those black eyes full of desire. She climbed on top of him and whimpered.

"I'm going insane."

He brought up an arm and stroked her back. "Part of the process. It hurts?"

"Yes! I can't stand it."

He didn't ask any further questions but hitched his hips and pulled her nightie up. His cock sank into her pussy, and she howled his name.

"Hard." She tried thrusting to get him deeper, but he held her still with one hand on her ass. With gentle movements, he glided to the hilt of his shaft and retreated. He pushed in again and let himself ease away. "No, not like that!"

"Shh, it's okay. Feel me," he soothed.

Shae punched his shoulder, almost sobbing. "You don't understand. I can't take it. I'm on fire. If you don't do it rough, I'm going to snap. I have to have it. I think I'm going to lose my mind."

He let her ramble on and on, but still he kept to his unhurried pace, making love to her rather than fucking the way she begged him to do. Why now did he find the control to be gentle when she needed his body like she needed air to breathe? He wouldn't let her move on her own or allow her to sit up so she could ride him like a show pony. He kept her sealed to his chest, using one arm as if she didn't warrant all his strength. She fought him and smacked his face. He rolled them on the bed until he was above her. He raised one of her thighs higher and sank deep into her pussy. She pleaded.

"Eiji, you're torturing me. I'm coming!"

An orgasm rocked her. Muscles in her core spasmed over and over again, and the thrill took her ability to speak. Eiji kept pumping, which was a good thing because the thirst hadn't died out. If anything, it grew worse. Her clit buzzed, sensitive and swollen. Her juices flowing didn't affect the tightness of her pussy. The walls clenched around his dick, milking it in a silent plea to be used and abused.

Eiji sat up and raised her legs. He clenched them at the backs of her thighs and pushed so her knees touched her shoulders and her ass came up off the bed. "Don't worry. I'm not going to stop."

She stared mesmerized as his cock disappeared between her nether lips and drew out, long and fat, before driving in again. His member glistened with her come, and the sight brought on a small aftershock of an orgasm. Still, her body refused to acknowledge satisfaction.

Eiji pulled out until just the tip of his dick pierced her. He paused, and she screamed. He drove forward at a snail's pace, but when he buried the extent of himself inside, he thumped tight against her opening. She keened and scratched at the sheets.

"Again," she pleaded.

He gave her what she wanted. For an hour he took her that way, in that position, never once breaking his rhythm. How? Was this the ability of just the wolf shifter or all of them? Eiji turned her to her side and closed her legs together. The move made him a snugger fit, and she moaned, giving in to the pleasure but needing more.

"W-Why?" She covered his hand with hers at her hip. He drove deep into her and took away her ability to resist. She lay open to him, exposed, his to do with what he chose. He leaned forward and let her feel some of his weight, heavy and hard. He curved above her length, sealing them together and grinding on her ass. Quakes went off in her belly and extended to her arms and legs. She came, but the orgasm was to such a degree that it knocked out reasonable thought. All she knew was him, the way he moved and the soft words he spoke as he pleasured her. Even when he lapsed into Japanese, he held her captive.

Somehow Shae knelt on her knees, ass in the air, head on the pillow. Packaging tore open, and a condom snapped into place. He hadn't used one all this time. "There's no danger," he said as if in answer to her mental question.

He curved over her length, and fingers found her wet pussy. She shuddered in ecstasy when he pushed them between her folds, coating his digits with her thick cream. He pulled out and wove into her anus. She clenched her teeth together and arched into his touch. Over and over he worked her back entrance, until her muscles loosened. Then he pulled his fingers free and threaded the tip of his cock into the narrow opening. She grabbed his wrist, and he paused. Her eyes shut, she felt his gaze on her, and then his lips touched hers. They kissed for long moments, their tongues curling together. He strummed her nipple with the pad of a thumb and whispered encouragement in her ear.

Holding her close as if she were a treasured gift, he eased deeper inside her, one slow inch at a time. Shae trembled. Her desire shot up a few degrees even as she didn't think it could get any hotter. This virus would kill her in the end but still leave her unsatisfied, feverish for more and more sex.

When Eiji seated himself to the hilt, he turned them both to their sides, and he snuggled behind her. Relaxed and tender, he made love to her from behind. She clung to his arms enfolding her middle and matched him thrust for thrust. Her ass pushed out, a thrill raced over her being each time he thumped her full to capacity.

"I think I can't...I can't get enough," she panted. "It won't stop. I want to come and come. Eiji—"

"Shh, I will satisfy you, Shae. *Yakusoku*. I promise."

* * * *

At seven in the evening, Shae left the bed and stood in the shower. Water hot as she could stand it ran over her skin. Her nipples pebbled, and her pussy clenched. Eiji had taken her until she'd fainted from exhaustion. He had lasted longer than her, and they'd gone on for hours. Still, right now the thirst burned. She faced the wall and flattened her hands on the surface before resting her forehead between them and shut her eyes. Not until the heat of his body warmed hers did she realize Eiji was there. His thigh brushed her ass. He touched her hips on both sides and nuzzled her neck.

Shae found his mouth and kissed him hungrily. After some time, they broke apart, both panting and staring into each other's eyes.

"Does he know about this too?"

"He does."

She turned to face him and traced droplets of water over his chest, down his belly, and into his crotch. His skin, so taut and warm beneath her touch, drew her lips to taste him. She dropped to her knees and kissed his thigh. The muscle twitched, and she licked the spot again. When she went after his cock, he drew her away and made her stand.

"Why won't you let me suck you?" she complained.

"Not now."

"Why?"

He lowered to his knees and drew her close. The next instant her legs were wrapped around his head, and he buried his mouth between them, eating her flowing juices. She rode his face, tangling her fingers in his hair with one hand and holding onto the wall with the other. Eiji brought her to multiple orgasms, and only when she threatened to faint again did he let her down. She stood in front of him, unmoving, while he washed her length, rinsed the suds away, and then lathered her skin again. When she smelled of a sweet but subtle fragrance, he cleaned himself and turned the water off. She left the shower cocooned in a thick white towel, held in his arms.

Shae sat on the bed lotioning her skin while Eiji made dinner. When he returned to the bedroom, they ate together in silence. She made no comment to the fact that neither of them had put on clothes, but since her wayward body simmered on low heat as if it intended to blaze up at any second, she thought he might accommodate her later.

Sometime after twelve it happened, and Eiji pulled her onto his lap, facing away from him. The bed squeaked on its springs for the rest of the night, and no sound punctuated the air in the room other than her and Eiji's moans for hours on end.

* * * *

"Do you mind? I have some business to take care of. I will come back."

Shae pounced on the excuse. She pushed Eiji toward the door. "Of course not. You can't just neglect yourself worrying about me." Even touching him the way she did, heat radiated through his shirt, and while it didn't set off the storm of lust from a week ago, she wanted him nearby. Her sexual drive had been back to normal for a while. She had bouts of sickness and weakness, but mostly she stood on an even keel. Despite that, every time she opened her eyes, her first thought was of Eiji. That couldn't be. She needed a break from him, wanted to get him out of the house because she'd been too dependent. "I'll be here."

He took a few steps toward the door, but hesitated. "Do you feel…"

Her throat dried. "Feel what?"

Dark eyes burrowed into hers as if he could read her soul. She turned her gaze away, hoping one of the abilities of the wolf shifters wasn't mindreading. He seemed at a loss on how to explain what he meant, or it could be he didn't want to bring it up. If that were the case, they were in agreement. The weirdness that sometimes arose inside worried her, but she also wondered if it wasn't just her crazy mind playing tricks on her. Every day, she still told herself this was some kind of elaborate joke or a dream that had gone on too long. Nothing extreme had happened beyond getting sick, and that just could have been infection from Darryl's psycho ass biting her.

"I'm fine, Eiji. Like I said, you don't have to worry about me. Go on. I want to be alone, and you've been getting on my nerves lately."

His brows rose, and she almost laughed. She refused to take back her words, and after he studied her a bit longer, he turned and left, the door clicking behind him.

Shae blew out a breath in relief and walked to the bedroom. She sat down on the side of the bed and glanced at the TV. No, the programs there didn't hold her. She liked to keep moving and having fun. Locked in the house all this time had worn on her emotional state, but thinking about going out scared her too. If Darryl had turned her agoraphobic, she'd kill him twice.

An odd thought popped into her head, or more like an odd desire. She suppressed it and picked up her cell phone. Her dad's number on speed dial, she phoned him and waited with a somersaulting stomach.

"Shae, dear," came her dad's deep tones over the line.

Rapt fear overtook her. What had she been thinking? If she wasn't human...

"I'm sorry I've missed your calls, honey, but as I said, I was arranging for someone trustworthy to reboot our systems. I think I found him. In fact, you can come home within the week. It looks like we recovered a small bit of data for a portion of Asia."

She had been tapping her fingers on the bedside table, but at his words, she stilled. "A-Asia?"

"Yes! That's the brilliance of our new boy. I shouldn't call him boy, but to me, you know..."

He rambled on. She thought about her mother and the new information Eiji had shared with her. Questioning her dad on the phone wasn't how she preferred to do it. She wanted to look into his eyes and demand to know the truth, but going home now could not happen. The niggling desire grew by several degrees.

"Dad, seriously, I haven't been here a month, and I haven't taken off for years. You can spare me a little longer, right?"

"Is something wrong, honey? You don't sound the same."

She clenched her teeth. "No, why would anything be wrong? I'm soaking up the sun, partying like there's no tomorrow, and well, the guys aren't half bad out here."

"Oh, Shae, when will you settle down? I've told you I want grandchildren."

An image of puppies popped into her head, and she almost sobbed. "I know, Dad. I'm just—"

"I know. Sowing your oats. Don't wait too long. You're over thirty now."

"Gee, thanks for pointing that out."

Her mother had always loved kids and had pushed for their father to have more after Shiya, but Dad had refused, given their dangerous work. As far as she knew, it was the only thing they had seriously disagreed on.

"Daddy, I know you're not turning me down for some rest, are you?"

"Don't you try to manipulate me, young lady," he snapped.

She sighed. "I will be on the road by morning."

"No, you will not." His tone softened. "Sakura is coming home. She will take anything that might come up. Honey, you come home when you're ready. I don't like you girls overworking yourselves."

Why did it sound like his idea that she take some more time? "Okay, Dad, thanks."

"What was it you called me about before?"

She licked her lips and eyed the dresses hanging in the closet. "Nothing. Just wanted to hear your voice. I'll call you later, okay? I love you."

"I love you too, honey. Bye."

He ended the connection. Shae stood up and walked to the closet. She sifted through the clothes she had hanging there and found the shortest dress, with a neckline that plunged almost to her navel, and tossed it on the bed. Afterward, she jumped into the shower. Twenty minutes later, she doused her erogenous zones with a scent that had burned her nostrils days ago. Tonight, it enticed. She did her makeup, curled her hair, and dressed. The five-inch strappy heels in place on her feet, she headed out of the house and slid behind the wheel of her car and headed into the night.

The club she drew up to was one she hadn't been to before, but after parking her car, she headed inside, confident of what she intended to do. She crossed to the bar and ordered a drink while surveying the crowd. Once she had it in hand, she took a sip and headed out to the dance floor. In the center, she drank some more and began swaying her hips to the rhythm of the music. Like bees to honey, the men swarmed around her, crowding closer, grinning and calling out to her. Even while the music blared at ridiculous decibels, she heard every word. They offered to buy her a drink, asked for a dance, begged to take her home. Still, she moved.

She shut her eyes and raised her arms in the air. Rough hands landed on her hips, and a hot body zipped in close behind. Another joined him from the front. Whoever these two men were didn't matter because they were replaced in seconds, dragged away by two new men. Shae downed the last of her drink and opened her eyes to choose a man. She handed him the glass with widened eyes and a pout. He disappeared. When he returned with another drink, she thanked him with a smile and took a sip. Clubbing 101 said don't take drinks from people one didn't know. She had taken the gift without a qualm, and just to tease all the guys at once, she stuck out her tongue and licked the rim of the glass, a slow circle, made to tantalize. Growls of lust and curses dropped from lips all around.

Shae played this game for a good half hour, and then the crowd parted—or rather, they were shoved aside. She stopped dancing and watched as Darryl's men thrust their way through the men surrounding her. Those who resisted found themselves on the floor after a fist to the face. She figured bouncers would appear at any second, but none showed up. Then Darryl stood before her. He didn't touch her, but he grinned as if she should be happy to see him.

"Hey, baby girl. How's it going?"

She closed the space between them and brought her hands up to his chest. As if they'd cued each other, they began to sway to the music at the same time. She stretched up on her toes, and he bent to accommodate her, planted a feather light kiss on her lips, and nuzzled along her neck. His deep breath told her he breathed her scent in, and she did the same. His was as familiar to her as if the two of them were one.

"You're looking hot as hell tonight," he whispered in her ear.

"Thanks." Pleasure permeated her system. She ran flattened palms up to his shoulders and linked her hands behind his head. He brought his arms around her waist and crushed her to him. His rough hold hurt a little, but she accepted it. Song after song played, but they never broke their slow rhythm. Shae kept her eyes closed most of the time, but when she opened them, it was to look into the angry face of a woman she recognized as one of the girlfriends of the others, maybe Travon.

Shae scoped her. Slender and black, she wore her hair long, almost to her waist, and her dress was so tight it must have cut off circulation in spots. Despite that, she looked good, if skanky, and anyone could see she had a problem with Shae.

"Why is she giving me the stink eye?" Shae commented.

Darryl leaned back. His hand had been steadily moving lower toward her ass, but when she spoke, he stopped and looked down at her. He followed the direction of her gaze and chuckled. "That's Charlene. Don't worry about her. She's Travon's girl. Jealous of how sexy you look tonight, I guess, but she'll respect you when you take your place as my queen."

Shae flinched at the use of the word and the position, but she didn't say anything.

One of the other girls grabbed Charlene's arm. "Come on. Let's hit the ladies' room real quick. You look like you could use a break."

Darryl grinned, still amused, and Travon strolled over to him. When they started talking, Darryl led her from the dance floor, and Shae stood at his side looking around. She sighed. "Hey, I'm going to go to the ladies' room too, okay?"

He waved his hand, not paying her any mind. "Yeah, whatever."

She left his side and headed toward the back of the club to a door with the word "Ladies" over the top. When she pushed through, she found Charlene and the other woman doing their makeup at the sink. Although the tiny room bulged at the seams with women, the two shifters had been given the space they needed.

Charlene rolled her eyes and touched up her lipstick. "Why are you in here? Come to show us how special you are?"

The other woman grabbed her arm. "Don't start, Charlene. You know Darryl won't like it."

"What, she think she all that. You can tell by looking at her."

Shae held her hands out to the sides. "Go ahead and look, girlfriend. I'm used to women hating on this."

"Bitch!"

Charlene lunged at her, but the other woman shouted, this time not touching Charlene. "Stop! I said back the hell off!"

The resentful gaze tossed at the other girl surprised Shae, but Charlene obeyed. Shae wondered if there was some kind of hierarchy involved with wolf packs. The other woman must have a higher position than Charlene, and from the looks of it, Charlene didn't appreciate it. She glared at Shae as if it were her fault.

"Don't think because all those guys were pushing up on you that you got it going on, 'cause you don't. That was Darryl."

Shae was about to dismiss her words, but paused at the mention of Darryl. "I don't know what you're talking about."

Charlene glanced at the other woman, and they both smiled. Charlene approached her. "Maybe you always come out half naked and drink whatever's put into your hand. Maybe you don't have a problem with how Darryl turned you against your will. Oh, yeah, we knew his plan. He doesn't do anything without talking to his boys about it."

Cold dread started at the base of Shae's skull.

When she said nothing, Charlene continued. "Then again, maybe the legendary Keiths aren't as badass as everyone hears they are. I know that bullshit about the women being beautiful isn't."

"Fuck you," Shae snapped, but without much heat. Thoughts swirled in her mind. If nothing else, the skank was right about her not behaving the way she usually did. She loved going out, and sometimes she bought dresses that were way beyond what she'd put on in public. They were for her and her man to enjoy at home. Tonight she'd slipped into one without a qualm and left the house to come to the club.

"It's all coming together for you, ain't it?" Charlene laughed. "Darryl made you, and he can make you do anything he wants. He can even get you to spread your legs right here in front of everybody and fuck you, and you'll love every minute of it."

"That's a lie!" Shae stumbled away from the gloating expressions on their faces. Eiji had said she had a choice. She could be Darryl's mate or his. He didn't mention anything else except that Darryl could force himself on her and make her his mate. But that meant rape, didn't it?

Shae spun on her heel and walked out of the bathroom. She

stopped, fear tightening her chest. If she went back over near Darryl, would it happen again? Would she just let that fool touch her wherever he wanted, however much he wanted? Bile threatened to rise up in her throat, and her hands shook. She edged around the room, away from Darryl, knowing at any time he could pick up her scent and know she wasn't in the bathroom. Her knees quivered. She darted her gaze everywhere, unable to focus on who stood in front of her. When a few men smiled, she just bit off a cry. This was too much. Never in her life had she ever felt so naked, and it had nothing to do with her clothes.

She made it to the exit and burst through the door. Cool night air ruffled her hair, smelling of the ocean. She breathed deep and stumbled away from the club's entrance.

Someone grasped her arm. "Ma'am, are you okay? Do you need me to call you a taxi?"

She shook off the hold. "I'm fine."

"I don't think—"

"Leave me the hell alone!" She punched him so hard he went flying backward off his feet. He landed wrong on the ground, and the distinctive snap of a bone breaking reached her over several people's gasps.

Shae slapped a hand over her mouth. *Oh no! I'm so sorry.* She fled, not even knowing where she was going. After a block, she yanked off her shoes and continued on. If she cut her feet, she didn't know it. Numb and confused, she kept moving. When she couldn't see, she realized she had been crying. That was another new one too. After some time, she looked at the street sign and saw Dell Avenue. This was one she recognized. A canal ran across this road. Sure enough, she came to the small bridge and turned into a narrow walk with heavy tree coverage over it. Beside her the canal streamed, softly rippling in the dim lighting. A row of manicured bushes separated the walk from the water, and at intervals were docks where people had moored small boats. She had no idea whether this was their backyards and if she was trespassing, but at the moment, she didn't care.

A shadow moved across the path up ahead, and she froze. Whoever it was made no move to come closer or to go in the opposite direction. She told herself to take a deep breath and ascertain whether the person was human or something else, but her chest burned holding it in. The shadow stirred, and her heart hammered in her throat. Somewhere nearby, a dog barked, and then another sound rent the air. Shae sank to the ground, her shoes slipping from numb fingers.

She dug her cell phone from the tiny purse she carried. Thank goodness she'd brought it. The display read "Eiji," and she almost wept anew.

"Eiji," she breathed.

"I'm at the house, but you're not here. You are not well enough to go out yet, Shae," he scolded.

She shut her eyes and tried to wet her dry throat. "He... he..."

"Shae!" This time his tone was sharp with concern. "Where are you? Is he there with you? Tell me everything."

"I'm somewhere on a canal street, near Dell. Eiji, he made me..." Horror washed over her, and she sank farther toward the ground. Having no idea where the shadow had gone or if someone stood over her ready to kill her, she clung to the phone, drawing strength from Eiji's voice. He seemed so close, yet so far away, and the desperate need to feel his comforting arms overwhelmed her.

"I will find you."

The phone went dead, and she yelped in alarm. Minutes ticked by, and each sound in the night banged loud in her ears. Something splashed in the water, making her jump. The dog's bark appeared closer, and a man's angry voice rose above it all, his abusive words to whomever he spoke grating Shae's raw nerves.

At any moment, Darryl might figure out she'd left, or Charlene and the other woman might tell him. He could track her and get there before Eiji. Could she resist the magic he'd used on her and fight him? Was the man she'd hurt giving her description to the police even now?

At the end of the short canal, someone flashed a light into the darkness. Her heart leaped in her chest. She fell backward onto her ass and scraped her leg on the asphalt. Two men spoke, and she imagined one had the authoritative air of a cop. She rolled to her knees despite the pain and scrambled for her shoes. A splash. Damn, now she realized what the first splash had been.

She took flight in the opposite direction from the men. Reaching the corner, she had to stop dead because of oncoming traffic in both directions. For the life of her, she couldn't figure out which way led back to the house. Maybe she shouldn't go there anyway. Darryl knew where she stayed, and he had more than enough people backing him up. Eiji would be no threat whatsoever.

A woman on the opposite side of the street watched her with leery eyes, and Shae started walking. She hoped the fact that she had no shoes on wasn't too obvious. People walked around in bathing suit tops and Daisy Dukes all the time out here, so being shoeless shouldn't be too much of a stretch.

A car inched past her and then came to a stop not far away. Drivers from others who couldn't get around in the narrow street laid on their horns. A man stuck his head out the window and looked her way, a black man. Shae stopped walking and backpedaled a few steps. She could call her protector—no, it wasn't fair to drag her family and their employees into a fight with wolf shifters and not tell them fully what they dealt with.

She couldn't explain what she was becoming, and besides that, Eiji might be caught in the crossfire. Despite everything, he had been good to her, and she didn't want him to die. *If anyone had told me a couple weeks ago I would want a shifter to live...*

"Hey, baby, need a ride?" the man shouted.

She raised her voice and heard the tremor when she spoke. "No, I'm good. Thanks."

The passenger door opened, and light-headedness assailed her.

"Don't be like that, pretty girl." The threat in his tone had to be her imagination. Not right here, where anyone could see her or hear her scream? Or was Darryl in the car waiting to use his ability to draw her, without a struggle, into its dark interior? All she had to do was scent him, but fear blocked everything, including common sense. She had no idea what to do. Instinct said run and don't stop. The man took a step toward her, still ignoring the cars lined up behind him. Shae stumbled when she stepped on a rock, and a steely arm encircled her waist. She started to scream.

"Easy," came Eiji's deep, commanding voice, and she sagged into his embrace.

The man from the car tossed out an insult she ignored and jumped back into his car. Soon traffic moved forward, but Shae clung to Eiji with all her waning strength.

"You lied," she muttered against his throat. "You said I had a choice."

"We'll talk about it when we get back to the house. Where are your shoes?"

"I don't know." Tired beyond reason, she couldn't muster more than a sulky answer and slapped his hands away when he tried to carry her. She followed him to his Jeep, parked nearby, and climbed into the passenger seat. By the time they reached her rental, which took no more than a few minutes, she was nodding in and out of sleep.

Eiji touched her cheek, and she jerked away. His mouth tightened. "What happened tonight?"

She left the Jeep and walked up the steps to the door. He came behind her and wrapped an arm around her waist to lift her aside and then unlocked the door himself. A cold chill ran along Shae's back, and she cast a glance into the street behind her, toward the bushes and in the shadows. Nothing stirred. The moon came out from behind some clouds to mock her. Where had its bright light been when she was alone on that canal road? Then again, the moon gave no comfort. The pale chunk of rock belonged to the wolves.

She stomped past Eiji in the entrance and went to the kitchen to find a drink. A glass with a splash of rum and pineapple juice and a few cubes of ice, and she found her backbone again. She slammed the glass on the counter and turned to Eiji just entering the room.

"Explain to me why I had to learn the hard way that Darryl can control me any damn time he's good and ready. Why didn't you warn me, and how can I fight it?"

He pierced her with those eyes, and she found herself wondering what he looked like shifted. "You can't fight it. Right now, you belong to him."

Chapter Eight

Eiji fought panic and rage. He smelled *him* all over Shae as if they'd lain together. She'd told him Darryl didn't have sex with her the night he bit her, and Eiji knew it to be true. He would have picked up the scent without trouble. However, now she carried a bit of the man inside her. She would always reek of his enemy unless she mated, and he had spoken the truth. She belonged to Darryl.

"Oh hell to the no! I'm not having that." She made herself another drink. He knew if he attempted to stop her, she would fight him, so he stood where he was. Her big brown eyes accused him, and that was enough to fuel his guilt. "You need to stop holding back, Eiji. Tell me everything, and don't start spouting that crap about making me your mate, because it's not going to happen."

He hitched his shoulders and moved to make tea. "Tell me everything that happened tonight."

"Isn't it obvious from this getup?" She snatched at her dress with derision curling her full lips and then, in an impulsive move, drew the offending garment over her head and threw it on the floor. Eiji's cock hardened with the first sight of her bare breasts and the scrap of material that was her panties. She didn't seem to notice how she affected him or whether it was appropriate for her to strip there in the kitchen. *American women.*

"Did he hurt you?" he broached to get her talking again.

"He humiliated me." And then she sniffed, fighting tears.

He threw the teakettle aside and shoved a chair from his path, overturning it. When he drew her into his arms, she came without a fuss, still struggling to remain strong. He carried her to the bedroom and held her tight to his chest. He wanted to go on holding her, but instead, he laid her down on the mattress and took a seat beside her. Shae gave him a look filled with hatred, and she climbed up the bed until she reached the headboard. She dragged a sheet and blanket with her and tucked them beneath her chin after she'd drawn her knees up to it.

"He had full control, and I didn't realize it. I thought I got a crazy idea in my head to go out and have some fun. I selected my clothes, my shoes, even where to party. Something should have told me this was all strange since I never even knew that place existed."

Eiji remained silent, allowing her to share her tale.

"I pushed up on him all night. I let him touch me as we danced. I would have gone further and done whatever he wanted, and now that I think about it, all his boys were laughing at me. The girls were jealous, maybe 'cause they wanted his low-life ass, but it was one of them that warned me about what was going on."

"How did you get out?"

Her eyes widened as she stared at him. "Wait, because I shouldn't have been able to? Is that what you're saying?" Before he could answer, she went on. "One of the guys had to talk to him about something. That took his attention, and he was done with me for the moment."

Eiji nodded. "To control another in his pack takes concentration of his power, and it does drain energy."

"Power?" Shae repeated.

He hesitated. Eiji had known all of this could happen, but he never expected it to happen before she made her choice. He knew he'd had a few more days before she changed for the first time and Darryl would return for her. He had hoped to have that time to explain the reality she faced.

"The alpha of a wolf pack has the ability to control his people to a certain extent, to influence them, to strengthen them, and even to heal them."

She gasped, and in her distraction, the sheets slipped. He couldn't stop his gaze from lowering to her bare breasts. The dark area around her nipples called to him to trace it, to taste her skin. He had never lain with an African American woman before, but Shae had quickly become an addiction, one he found no reason to deny himself. That is, unless she mated with Darryl. He could not let that happen, even if he did tell her she had a choice.

"You're telling me an alpha wolf can make people do whatever he wants? That's...that's..." Her chest rose and fell at a rapid pace, and her lips parted, her voice weak as if she had to force it to work.

"Not any people," he corrected. "Only his pack."

"I'm not in his damn pack!"

"But he did make you."

"Make me!"

"Shae, shouting will not help us find the solution."

She rolled her eyes at him and rose from the bed to find a nightie to pull on. The decision gave him relief and disappointment. "He made me like y'all, so he can throw me around like a rag doll. Can you do that to me too? Is that why you and I did—"

"No!" He blew a breath out through his nostrils and spoke with more reserve. "I told you. I am a rogue. I do not have a pack. I am not an alpha."

She put a hand on her hip, considering him. "But you do have the power of one, don't you?"

He refused to answer that question. "You are correct. You are not a member of his pack, so he controls you only because he made you, and there was a level of intimacy started between you." Eiji ground his teeth. "When you are fully wolf, he will have the ability to mark you as his mate and claim you."

"Which means?"

"You walked away from him tonight because you wanted to. As his mate, you won't want to."

The bathroom door slammed shut, and the lock clicked into place. Eiji banged on the door, but she refused to answer. He picked up the sound of retching, and he shut his eyes, resting his forehead on the chilly wooden panel. No matter how many times he called out her name, she ignored him.

After some time, the toilet flushed, and the faucet water ran. The low *shoosh* of a toothbrush being used started up, and then more water. She gargled, and the shower turned on. All the time, he waited, listening for sniffs or sobs. There were none. He'd known from the first time he met her she was strong. Yet, often he thought there was more to her, something beyond normal American women. He couldn't be sure, and she hadn't shared all regarding her family. He had seen the hesitation whenever the subject arose. He considered it rude to push and waited for her to trust him. If she had done so earlier, tonight would not have happened. Still, he couldn't blame her.

A new scent met him, and a low growl began in his throat. He took another second to listen in on Shae's movements and then left the house. Not fifty feet away, the beast waited. Eiji shut the door and walked into the shadows. The brown wolf was nothing special, big body, conical head, and shorter legs. He bared his teeth at Eiji and crouched low as if ready to attack, but Eiji didn't sense the intent to kill, at least not at the moment.

They stared into each other's eyes a long time, assessing. Eiji didn't risk looking away. He knew the wolf would take it as him giving place or as fear. Even if he didn't mean to attack, he would do so because he thought he had the advantage. Eiji would not give him the opportunity.

"Change," Eiji commanded, growing tired of the game. "You have something to say. *Hai?*"

The wolf gave a low, annoyed yip, and then he did shift to a human form. Eiji recognized him right away, although he had known before now. Travon, the third in Darryl's pack.

"What do you want?"

Travon spit on the ground in front of Eiji. "I came with a message from Darryl."

Eiji waited in silence.

"He wants to thank you for taking care of his girl." The grin that spread over the man's face said the words were far from gratitude. "You've done a good job. You got her over the hump when our kind risks dying. A lot of our women die before…" For a few seconds, real emotion appeared in his eyes, and then it disappeared. "Darryl says keep your hands off her now. Don't even think about having sex with her because he'll know if you do, and you'll find yourself dead like your cousin."

Eiji stilled. "What do you know of Izumi?"

Travon waved a hand like that wasn't important, but Eiji stormed him and whipped the man off his feet, holding him by the neck. Two strides forward, and he slammed Travon against the tree behind him. Travon's feet dangled inches off the ground. He tried prying Eiji's hand from his throat, but failed.

"Answer," Eiji spat. His eyes burned a little with the change because his anger had erupted, and fine white hairs skimmed along his arms. If he wasn't careful, he would shift to the white wolf, the form most of the women in his family took on.

He squeezed Travon's neck, and the man gasped and gurgled for air. "I-I c-can't tell if I c-can't breathe."

Eiji let him fall to the ground, and Travon rolled to his knees, rubbing his neck and panting. He glared up at Eiji while he crouched. "You're going to pay for that shit."

"My cousin," Eiji repeated.

Travon took his time standing. "I don't know nothing. Just that she died, and she was one of us."

Eiji's eyes widened. "In your pack?"

"No, never!" His gaze grated up and down Eiji. "Why would we want...Anyway, I meant wolf. She was there back at that house, and then she died."

"I don't believe you."

"I don't give a fuck, Chinaman."

Eiji gritted his teeth. "I am Japanese."

Travon shrugged. "You got the message. Follow what Darryl says. He's not good with people crossing him."

Eiji had had enough. He poked a finger in Travon's chest and strode closer. "You tell your alpha to stay away from Shae. She's a good girl. She doesn't need your kind of trouble, but she will decide what she wants. I will stay by her until she knows what that is."

He thought his declaration would anger the brown wolf shifter, but instead Travon threw his head back and laughed long and loud. Eiji hitched his shoulders, eager to do more than threaten. The violence that rose in his chest pushed him to want to demonstrate his strength using Travon and send him back to Darryl in a body bag. Still, he needed to remember who he was.

He enforced the law. He didn't break it, even if he was in another country. His headquarters often worked with the United States' law enforcement agencies, and he would not bring shame on his superiors by behaving dishonorably away from home.

"You don't even know what kind of woman you're taking care of, do you?" Travon taunted. "You don't know who she is?"

Eiji growled. "Not a good idea to insult her character in front of me."

Travon whistled. "Damn, man, you got it bad. Her pussy must be tight."

The relaxed hand at Eiji's side connected in a fist with Travon's chest. The man stumbled backward and crashed into the tree before sliding down its trunk to the ground. His eyelids fluttered, and his head lolled on his neck as he tried pulling out of the disorientation. Eiji stooped and rested his forearms on his thighs, steepling his fingers.

"Is there something else?"

Travon tried glaring, but his gaze wasn't focused. When he spoke, it was with slurred words, but Eiji already saw the swift healing taking place, native to shifters of all kinds. That was why he hadn't held much back during the hit. He could have crushed the man's chest cavity, but that would incite a war, one he might not win with no one behind him.

"She's a Keith," Travon said in a raspy tone. "You've heard of them?"

A cold breeze raised goose bumps on Eiji's arms and along his back. "Keith."

"Yeah, shifter hunters. *Killers*."

Eiji had heard of the them. They had not touched his family personally and had no extensive work in his country as far as he knew, but even his superiors had heard of them and speculated about bringing the Keiths to justice should a threat rise in Japan. The belief in people who could shape-shift in Japan came from a different perspective, he imagined, than in America. The Keiths were murderers in most Asian eyes, no matter their cause, and this man was telling him Shae was one. Shae—the woman he had intended to bring home as his mate.

"Tell me about Izumi," he said. "Did you kill her?"

"No."

"Your alpha?"

"Look, I don't know anything about that, like I said. I just know she died. She wasn't one of ours, so we didn't look out for her."

Eiji had come to America to bury his cousin. Her instructions were not to be transported back to Japan. She had become like these people, caring more for becoming a star and obtaining wealth and recognition than about family. By rights, Eiji should have turned his back on her as well, the way his family had. He had kept his distance, but never broke contact. Always, he had hoped Izumi would see reason and come home. Now it was too late. She had died alone with no one around her to help guide her spirit to its resting place or to pray for her.

Eiji heaved a sigh and dismissed the dark thoughts. Izumi had made her choices, the same as he, to live apart. Although she hadn't had the challenges nor the stigma of being born in dishonor. He didn't think of himself as less, just different, and he'd had thirty-three years to come to terms with what he was.

When he could, Travon worked to stand. He swayed on his feet, his jaw tight, obviously embarrassed that Eiji had gotten the best of him. Something told Eiji this would not be the last time they faced off. "Don't touch her."

Eiji worked to keep from knocking Travon on the ground again. "What does Darryl want with Shae if she is, like you say, a Keith? They are enemies of the wolf."

Travon grinned. "That's for Darryl to know and you to mind your own fucking business. Like I said, don't touch the girl. Just get her through the change, and we'll come for her. If you even try to take her out of Venice, we'll know, and you will be sorry. Hm, maybe you'll be sorry either way."

"I do not accept threats. Darryl will have to deal with the consequences of what he did to Shae."

"You threatening my alpha?" Travon's chest swelled, and he bared sharpened teeth, but he made no move to approach Eiji.

"No, I'm not."

Travon laughed. "In the end, you're just a pussy. You know who's strongest around here. We've got ten guys in our pack, plus the girls, and at any time, Darryl can call in favors if he needs to. Who you got?"

He hesitated. Sometimes in his line of work, he needed to bluff in order to make the bad guy think he had a whole team behind him, but this was not the situation for that. He sensed the better move was to allow Darryl to think he stood alone and weak. That way his strength would be overlooked and underestimated. He already knew what would happen if Shae did not choose to mate with him. She had lied about who she was and continued to. She knew why Darryl wanted her, and it was not just because of her incredible beauty.

Eiji turned on the balls of his feet and started back toward the house. Travon shouted after him, but he pushed his hands into his pockets and continued on. When he reached the door, he listened and sniffed to see if he'd been followed, but the wolf shifter had left the area. Eiji figured they had a bit more time. Darryl would not approach Shae until she was fully wolf. The danger to her turning did not lie in death now, but in finding her right mind during the change. The aggression of the wolf could overtake her human side, and she could be no more than a vicious killer. In that case, he would have to put her down.

He let himself in the house. Shae stood in the kitchen at the refrigerator. She'd changed into shorts and a T-shirt and stared into the box, unseeing. Her toes curled on both feet as if in defense against the chill or life in general. She appeared more vulnerable than he'd ever seen her. Both desire and a need to protect her rose in him. He looked away and walked to right the chair he had knocked over earlier. After retrieving the teakettle, he started to make some and decided he wanted something stronger. His cousin had left a stock of both sake and wine. He took down a bottle of the sake, along with a glass from the cupboard, and had a seat. Two glasses swallowed, he poured a third and took his time.

"So your name is Shae Keith."

Chapter Nine

The room did a flip at Eiji's simple words and then righted itself. She continued to stare into the refrigerator. After a moment, she removed bread, mayo, mustard, and meat and cheese and set them on the table. Hunger was the farthest thing from her mind. How had he found out? What did it mean for their friendship and his helping her through the madness of becoming a shape-shifter? Denial didn't occur to her. Eiji's words weren't a question. At the same time, they weren't an accusation. She detected no emotion at all, not anger, not surprise. How the hell did she take him? No man confused her about what he thought or felt like Eiji did, and it drove her insane.

"Yes, it is," she said in answer to his question of her name.

"Darryl wants you as his mate."

"To somehow rule my family. I don't pretend to know the inner workings of his plan. Maybe he thinks he can change us all, one at a time, before anyone is the wiser. We can't all be his mate, can we? I mean us girls?"

He watched her, and something told her he was trying to

figure out why she wasn't defending herself or her family's ideals. She refused to.

"No. Just one."

"Lucky me." She put down the knife she'd been using to spread mayo on her sandwich and sighed. "Look, I'm not going to pretend I haven't done the things I did. Since you don't seem surprised or confused about learning my last name, I assume you've heard the details of what we do. We…"

Damn, it was hard to say for the first time. She licked her lips and stole a glance in his direction. He stood with his feet apart, arms folded. His expression appeared grim, but closed off. The warmth and gentleness she'd received at his hands and in his words during her sickness had evaporated into thin air.

"*I've* killed shifters…with my own hands. I believe—*believed*—they were abominations that don't deserve to live on this earth. Damn, I sound self-righteous or like some religious nut. The truth is I'm not sure I don't still feel that way. Look at what Darryl did to me and what nine times out of ten he'll probably do to others."

"Kill yourself."

She had brought her sandwich to her lips to bite for lack of anything better to do. At his words, she choked and coughed because the food went down the wrong pipe. Her eyes watered, and she blamed the pain in her throat rather than welling emotion. "Excuse me?"

She peered into his eyes and caught a flash of anger. "I said if you feel you are an abomination, one that will only hurt humans, who are better than you and more deserving of life, kill yourself. It is honorable."

"Don't give me that honor bullshit," she screamed. "I have a right to—"

"What?"

The sandwich thumped the bottom of the trashcan where she'd thrown it, and she cleaned up her mess, slamming jars on shelves and banging the refrigerator door shut. "I don't know! Why aren't you telling me how much you hate me now that you know? Why aren't you trying to kill me in retribution for all your brothers my family slaughtered?"

"It is not for me to kill you."

She put her hands on her hips. "What is that supposed to mean?"

He shrugged.

"Forget you. I don't need you, Eiji. I can take care of myself."

She dragged the trash bag from the can and started past him. Her shoulder bumped his arm, and his hand snaked out to capture her wrist. She found herself forced to face him, the bag slipping from her fingers. Eiji thumped her against the wall. Before he could bring a hand to her throat, she knocked it away and punched him in the face. She thought he'd block the hit, but he took it full on. She almost laughed at the surprise when his head snapped back on his neck. The impact gave her time to attack a second time, this one with her knee. He moved without effort and lightning fast. One hand covered the other to push her knee back down. Shae's legs gave, but Eiji caught her and pulled her close. She shoved against his chest.

"How long are we going to play this game?" she demanded.

"I am aware of no game."

"You know what I mean, Eiji."

"You have a decision to make."

When she wiggled in his hold, he let her go. She took two steps back, but not too far, so he wouldn't feel the need to come after her again. "I'm guessing being your mate isn't on the table anymore now that you know who I am."

He didn't say a word.

"That's what I thought." She stifled the hurt even though she had turned his high-handed solution down. "Am I going to be attacked again for taking out the trash?"

"I did not attack you."

"Whatever."

Eiji stepped around her and picked up the trash bag. She watched him walk to the door and then turned toward the bedroom. Apparently, she was to be held hostage a little longer.

That night, when she lay in bed, she expected Eiji to join her, but he never came into the bedroom. She knew he was still in the house because she smelled him, and if she listened hard, she could pick up the quiet breaths he took as he slept. Loneliness and rejection tasted bitter in her mouth. Eiji had felt like the only person she had on her side, but he had been there because he didn't know the truth. Now he did, and while he didn't walk away, he wasn't there either.

Sleep took its time coming, and when it did, she tossed and turned so much, she woke up repeatedly. By morning, the agitation of the previous night drove her to get out of the house. She showered and dressed in a bikini and sundress with flip-flops. She waited until Eiji occupied the shower and then left the house, headed toward the beach. Rather than walk the boardwalk, she continued to the warm sand and on to the water. Freezing cold, the waves came in to cover her feet. When the squishy sound her flip-flops made jarred her raw nerves, she took them off and walked along holding them.

After some time, an odd feeling came over her. She stopped and looked around. Darryl stood not ten feet away, and bile rose in her throat.

"Good morning, baby."

"Kiss my ass. I know what you did to me, Darryl, and it's not going to work."

He laughed and strolled toward her as if he had all day to get there. "If I wanted, I could have you stripped and spread for me right here for all the world to see."

"And the moment you let me go, I will cut your throat."

He waggled a finger and chuckled again. "I like your fight. It's going to feel good to break you."

"No man can break me."

"Oh yeah?"

He came closer, and for no reason at all, she laid a hand on his chest. To her utter horror, her pussy clenched in longing for this bastard. She fought with everything inside, to the point that beads of sweat broke out on her top lip and rivulets of moisture ran down from her temples. Darryl nipped at her chin with his teeth, a playful move as if they were lovers, teasing each other.

"You shouldn't challenge me, baby girl. You'll always lose."

"I hate your guts."

"I can even make you say you love me."

Panic stirred in her stomach. "If that's how you get your rocks off. Maybe no woman has ever been willing. You must be proud."

"Bitch," he growled.

He grabbed her chin and squeezed so hard she cried out. She tried doing to him what she'd attempted with Eiji, but this time she couldn't even raise her leg, let alone connect her knee with his balls. Darryl ground his mouth over hers, pressing hard until she tasted blood. She cried out and fought to get free from his hold. All she managed was to dig her nails into his arms, but she did all she could to cut into his flesh. He grunted in pain and shoved her back. She lost her footing and fell hard on the ground. Not even waiting for him to take control again, she flipped over to squat on her hands and feet and kicked out. Her foot connected with his leg, and the big bad wolf went down.

Darryl snarled his rage. He was on her in seconds and flattened her in the sand. If the soft grains hadn't provided a cushion, she would be dead or unconscious. Even so, her neck and shoulders ached with the strain of protecting herself. Darryl knotted fingers in her hair and yanked. She cried out.

"Hey!" someone called, but Darryl ignored the person.

He ran a hand up her thigh, raising her dress. He paused at the mound of her pussy, and she almost threw up in her mouth. Gathering a bunch of sand in her hand, she prepared to rub it in his eyes, but he anticipated her move and squeezed her wrist until she lost all feeling in her fingers.

"Miss, are you okay?" Hairy, pale legs stopped in her peripheral vision. Shae opened her mouth to say she wasn't okay, but Darryl's face made her pause.

His eyes shifted to the wolf's, and his canine teeth lengthened and sharpened while his muzzle protruded just enough to freak out any human who had the misfortune of seeing it. She didn't have to guess what he had in mind.

"You protect the humans, right? Wonder what this one will taste like." His laugh was low and throaty. "I vote it will taste like chicken."

"You wouldn't do that. You'd risk exposing your kind, and none of the shifters want that."

"Ma'am?" the man called out again.

Darryl leaned down and licked her neck. She just managed not to gag. "You mean *our* kind. What you gonna do, Shae?"

"I'm fine," she called out. "We just got a little frisky. It's all good."

Darryl's growl rumbled against her skin. Hatred choked her and curled her fingers in his shirt when she wished it was his throat. He'd manipulated her without using his power, showing just how low he could sink.

"You heard her," Darryl snapped, his face normal again as he glared up at the human. "Get lost and let me enjoy my girl."

The man stumbled backward and frowned. "You two should get a room. No one wants to see that."

"Not my fault you can't get laid," was Darryl's smart-ass reply. The man stomped away, leaving her trapped with no idea how she would escape. Darryl tugged at her panty line and snapped it against her ass. He laughed when she jumped. "Where was I?"

He lay on top of her with one leg between hers, the weight of the other crushing her into the sand. She switched their positions. He howled when she thumped his balls as she flipped him to his back. Not even looking for her flip-flops, she kicked off to get away, but he caught her hair and snatched her down. Sand filled her mouth, mixed with more blood.

"Where you going, bitch?" He moved above her again.

"No!" Something icy cold and then scorching hot zipped through her entire body. She didn't know where the strength came from, but the next instant, she threw Darryl into the water.

Somewhere nearby, a woman gasped. "Wait, did she just throw him?"

"We must be imagining it," her companion answered. "I knew people were crazy out here on the West Coast. It's too early for this, and I was drinking all night."

"Yeah," the first woman agreed. "We must be still hung over. Let's go back to our room."

Shae heard all of this conversation while keeping her eyes on Darryl. She crouched and bared her teeth. Adrenaline pumped through her veins, and the most insane longing to sink her teeth and claws into Darryl came over her. She took a slow step in his direction.

"Stop, Shae, you can't turn now." He seemed genuinely worried, but she didn't care.

"Run," she begged and was surprised at the deepness of her tone. Another step closer.

"Listen to me, damn it!"

"Run!" She leaped at him, but from nowhere Eiji was there between them. She screeched and tried to bite him. When that didn't work, she dug her fingernails into his arms, surprised and pleased at how long they extended.

"Not here, Shae." Eiji held onto her, but she had eyes only for Darryl and him alone. To kill him.

"Shae, calm down."

Heat flooded her body until she thought the world had turned red. "Why are you stopping me, Eiji? You hate him too. I want him dead now!"

"Look at me."

She pulled away from his hands as they framed her face.

"Shae, if you turn before the full moon, you will lose yourself."

"Lies!" She smacked at his face, but he caught her hand and folded her arm across her body. He enfolded her in his embrace, and all she could do was kick out at the air. She wriggled in his hold and stared at her enemy, so close and yet so far.

"Go," Eiji commanded Darryl.

"Who you think—"

"Go! You know what will happen if she changes now. She won't be able to be anyone's mate."

"She's mine. If anyone's going to make her calm down, it's me." Darryl took a step toward them, and Shae's teeth sliced into her bottom lip. Darryl froze and then fell back. He landed on his ass, and the shallow waves buffeted him. "I'll be back in six days."

Eiji turned from him as if he hadn't spoken. He spun Shae in his arms and trapped her face once again between his hands. "Shae, *kiku*. Listen. You must calm down."

She scratched at him and shook her head. Blind rage and hate dominated her thoughts. All she wanted was to kill, and since Darryl's scent faded with each passing moment, maybe she should focus on Eiji. Then again, hunting Darryl might give her satisfaction. From a great distance, Eiji called out to her, his tone insistent, but she swatted at the sound, waving her hand.

"Why are you here? Let me go!" She managed to break from his embrace only to have him pounce on her to flatten her in the sand.

"People are watching. Do you really want to talk here?" he demanded.

"They can witness me kick your ass." She snapped her teeth together in a sneer, but he appeared unimpressed.

"*Gomen.*"

"What do you mean you're sor—"

He grasped a small one-inch area on her wrist like he was checking for a pulse. A flash of feeling, as if cold water rushed up her arm, came over her. Before she could react, Eiji moved his hand to a point near her elbow and then ended with a swift, light tap to her temple. A burst of white light hit behind her eyes, and all went dark. His name exploded in her mind as she lost consciousness.

* * * *

When Shae came to, Eiji knelt over her patting the area at her nape. She rested her forehead on his chest, and the memory of what he'd done came back, except without the rage.

"Just breathe," Eiji instructed.

"W-What did you do to me, you bastard?" Her words held no heat. She managed to push his hand away and look up at him. The red tint over her eyes had gone, and while she didn't run her tongue over her teeth, she was pretty sure they were normal.

"Come. I'll take you back to the house."

"How long was I out?"

He didn't answer, but raised her to her feet. Shae resisted him carrying her, but he held a firm arm around her waist. Within a short time, they arrived at the house, and she sighed in the cool interior. She shoved him away, and he let her.

"Answer me, Eiji. What did you do?"

"I helped you to calm down."

"Yeah, because I wouldn't obey you. Is that it?" She put a hand on her hip.

"I did what was necessary. I'm sorry."

"You keep saying that, but somehow I don't think you even give a fuck. About me or anybody. Certainly not since you found out I'm a Keith. I'm surprised you even showed up at the beach." She spun on her heel and walked toward the bedroom, and he followed. "But don't even worry about it. I'm over this mess. I'm doing things the way we always do them, the way I should have from the beginning. I always have someone watching my back and making sure I'm not hurt."

She caught the jump in his jaw muscle and the narrowing of his eyes, but that didn't stop her from punching in the number on her cell phone. When the voice on the other end came on the line, she frowned. "Joe, where's Ace? I need him."

"He's indisposed. I'm at this number right now. What do you need, Shae?"

She hesitated. "Indisposed" usually meant one of their members was either injured or dead. Ace was her protector, and they'd been lovers for a time. "He's not…?"

"He'll be fine. Again, what do you need, Shae?"

She bit her lip. Joe was good at what he did, but he was also her sister's ex-boyfriend, and in Juneau, he'd made plain that he wouldn't mind starting something up with her. She'd put the asshat in his place and laid the matter to rest, but did he still have notions? The tone of his voice said business, but that could be a ploy.

"I need a protector, and I need a team. I have…"

Eiji laid a hand on hers. His dark gaze bore into her, cutting her deep despite the harsh way he'd treated her earlier. "Don't. I will look after you."

Shae shook his hand off. She had time. Darryl had said it himself. Six days. Her family could swoop in and wipe out Darryl and his pack before anyone was the wiser about her being no longer human. They deserved it, but she would still not tell them about Eiji. Then she could disappear somewhere far away. At the thought, her throat closed, and she had to take a moment to clear it before she spoke again.

"There's a wolf pack here. They need to be dealt with. I need a protector and a team. How soon can I get help?"

"By sunrise," Joe snapped. "Are you sure about this? Are you safe? If you need me to, I can drive over tonight. The rest can come behind me. You haven't been made, have you?"

She licked her lips and glanced at Eiji. No doubt he heard every word Joe spoke. "No, I haven't. I'm safe for now. The morning is fine. Um, please don't…uh…Don't bring Kasen. I want to handle this on my own."

He chuckled. "I know about doing everything you can to impress the higher-ups, and this would be huge. We've never brought down a wolf pack. Okay, in the morning then. Call me if you need me. I'll be there for you, no problem."

The warmth in his tone gagged her, but she thanked him all the same and ended the call. Her stomach knotted knowing she had to face Eiji and his possible wrath. She threw her shoulders back and raised her chin. "You don't agree with this, but it's the only solution I see."

"I suggested—"

"Please, that wasn't a suggestion, and you know it. I'm not going to be forced to be with a man, even if he is a decent guy." She met his gaze and saw his confusion. Of course he didn't get it. They were from two different worlds. "You heard everything. I don't want them to find out you're one of them and kill you. Even if you and I don't say anything, there's no guarantee Darryl or his people won't. I wouldn't put it past them to be that spiteful."

While she spoke, Eiji went about the room gathering clothes. At first she thought he intended to take her word and leave. The vise in her chest and the burning in her eyes were not to be examined. Then he brought out her suitcase from the closet and tossed it without ceremony on the bed. He dumped drawers full of clothing into it without folding them.

"What in the hell are you doing?"

He kept moving until she grabbed his arm and yanked a blouse from him. He dropped his hands on her shoulders. "You do not understand, Shae."

"Enlighten me!"

"Did you forget what happened on the beach?"

"I didn't forget how you karate chopped me upside the head."

Amusement lit his dark gaze, and she smiled. He pulled her close, and she let him lead her to his chest. She hated how much she wanted him, but the fact that he hadn't walked away meant he didn't totally reject her, knowing she was a Keith. Still, it didn't mean they had a future. He would not take her home to his mother. *Why am I even thinking about that? I'm going my own way.*

"Shae."

She looked up at him and felt something stir in her belly— desire and longing. She wanted to kiss him and hear him speak soft words of encouragement in his language even if she didn't know the meaning. For all her bravado, this situation scared the hell out of her, and she wasn't sure what the right path was. At any second, Darryl might ignore his promise to wait six days. Why that length of time?

Eiji answered her unspoken question. "The full moon is in six days. You will change for the first time."

"Well, that's plenty of chance to get rid of Darryl and his crew. Trust me. You don't know how good my people are. We can have this mess cleaned up in a jiffy." She fell silent. After this, there'd be no more involvement. She might even have to change her name to stay alive. The thought of never seeing Shiya and Sakura again, not to mention her dad, broke her heart.

"Shae." He caressed her cheek, and she turned into his touch, surprised at the tears in her eyes. Blinking them away, she sniffed and moved out of his hold.

"I'm fine."

"We're going."

"I just told you—"

He stopped her from dragging her clothes from the suitcase. For a few minutes, they fought, her trying to unpack while he dumped in more stuff.

"I'm not going to be bullied!"

"I'm not used to a woman like you. *Goujou na.*"

"Let me guess. Stubborn?"

He made an affirmative sound, and she put her hands on her hips. "Well, get over it. I'm not one of those women who just fall in line with whatever her man tells her. I have a mind, and I've been taking care of myself a long time. So you can go fuck yourself if you don't like it."

She spun away on her heel, but he came up behind her and dragged her back. She kicked out at his leg, but she might as well have been fighting a brick wall for the reaction it got. Her foot throbbed, and the jarring pain raced up her calf. She cursed him some more.

"Get your hands off me."

"Shae."

"Don't even speak my name. I'm done with you. I—"

"What do you think is going to happen when you get too angry tomorrow? Or when one of your people is killed or even hurt at the hands of one of the shifters? You have to wait until a full moon to change for the first time, and only with the help of one strong enough to lead you. Darryl and all the rest can change at will. They are the most vicious of the shifters, and they *will* kill your people. Look at what happened to you at the beach."

Shae stopped struggling. "If I do it early, then I can put it behind me and…"

"And go insane."

"How do you know that? I might be different. You said yourself you're different from your family members. Maybe American wolf shifters aren't like that."

"Then why did Darryl agree to wait?"

Defeat slumped her shoulders. "What are you suggesting?"

He stroked her arms, and she did all she could not to let it excite her. She failed miserably. Her pussy clenched and moistened. If she could smell her want, he could as well. She shut her eyes, feeling herself sway toward him, but standing rigid so as not to allow her body to brush his. How could a woman want a man as bad as she wanted him? Even when Darryl controlled her desires and made her hot, it wasn't like this. *Eiji.* Damn it all, she could chant his name. Why did she have to meet him? Why *him*? When he left…

A voice inside her head cried out, *"No!"*, and she wondered if it was her awakening wolf.

"Go somewhere safe with me. Wait it out. When it's your time, I will guide you."

To cover her weakness, Shae put a hand on her hip and tilted her head to the side. "How do you know you're strong enough? I mean, after all, you're just a rogue wolf, right?"

She didn't expect him to change. One minute he stood in her bedroom fully dressed. The next he shifted in a smooth, almost magical transition. He bent forward so his hands touched the floor, and as he did, his composition melted and reshaped. Hair sprang from every pore while his clothes fell away. Shae's jaw went slack at the huge white wolf standing before her. Pale gray eyes blinked at her, daring her to question his ability to handle his business. Any other time, she'd feel that familiar tightness in the pit of her stomach when she came face-to-face with a shifter, because these weren't mere animals. They could reason like a human and were multiple times stronger than their animal counterparts. Eiji didn't instill fear in her. She didn't know if it was because she was now like him—or almost so—or if it was because of the man himself.

"You're beautiful." She dropped to her knees and found her head lower than his. "Damn, you're huge."

She scratched the spot just beneath his ear and nuzzled her face into his fur. Eiji bumped her away with his nose toward the suitcase, and she sighed.

"Fine. I'll go." She stood and began repacking her things. Could she set her family on Darryl and his people? They were more family now. Was it wrong, and what about Eiji?

"You have to call and tell them not to come."

She jumped at Eiji's voice just behind her, but she didn't turn around because she hadn't heard him put his clothes back on. If she saw his naked body, she'd jump him, and they would get nowhere tonight.

"I don't know what I'm going to tell them, especially since I confirmed there are wolves here."

"Think of something."

She glared over her shoulder at the cold demand.

"We're not going to be here. You can't tell me you give a fuck about Darryl."

Eiji slipped into his pants and pulled them over lean hips. Shae enjoyed the view of the solid abs with rippled muscle. "When the time is right, I will kill him. The others only if they get in my way, but that is between us, not the humans."

She gaped at his calm statement.

"Your people *will* be hurt or killed, and that will hurt you. Call them."

"Eiji—"

He left the room with her suitcase. She flipped him off and then called Joe. She might not like it, but Eiji was right. Her family had to be warned off for just a little while.

A short time later, they were on the road. The house Eiji drove her to was located in the Hollywood Hills. The steep drive up to the house was long and winding, and the first appearance of the place sparked excitement in her belly. This was more along the lines of what she was used to. A multilevel structure with smooth white stone walls on the outside, small palm trees brought out the Western design along with strategic backlighting. When she stepped inside, she found more opulence and design to coax away the stresses of the day. An entire back wall was made of glass, and beyond it, an area held relaxing furniture, a built-in hot tub, and an unobstructed view of the city.

"You're renting this?" she asked Eiji.

His hand tightened on her suitcase handle, and his face reddened. "Izumi owned it. I rented one house and chose the other to live in."

"You got the better one."

He frowned. "Because it was taken first."

She laughed. "Uh-huh. She must have been doing well for herself. I don't blame old girl. I'm sure we can make do."

Chapter Ten

S ometime in the night, Shae woke in a panic. She sat up breathing hard and threw her legs over the side of the bed. No sounds reached her in the house other than the distant traffic. Even that would have been muffled out for a human.

The opposite side of the bed stretched cold and unruffled. Eiji had shown her to this bedroom and chose another for himself. He gave no indication of wanting to share a bed with her, and she didn't try to seduce him. Yet, fear had gripped her in her sleep, a terror that she heard Darryl calling her name. Now that she sat awake, nothing tugged on her conscience. No overwhelming need drove her to leave the house.

Padding barefoot, she left the room and walked out to the terrace. A cool breeze stirred her short curls and brought goose bumps to her legs beneath her nightie. She crossed her arms over her chest when her nipples peaked in the late-night air. A familiar scent stirred her senses. Fingers touched her belly from behind.

"You're shaking. If you're cold, come inside."

Why did Eiji's voice alone help her to deal with this mess of her life?

"I'm not cold."

His lips touched the delicate spot behind her ear. "He is not here, and he won't come."

"I might—"

"No. I will protect you."

"Eiji." She faced him and pressed into his throat. "Can you stop me if he calls?"

"I can."

She licked her lips and stared down at his chest. He smelled of soap, and his skin was warm, combatting the coolness of the night. She desperately wanted to believe him. What she wanted more was to trust herself, to know no one could make her do anything she didn't want to, but Darryl had proven her wrong twice, and it had stolen her confidence. This wasn't her, and it took everything inside not to crumble into a weeping idiot.

"What would it mean to become your mate?" she ventured.

Eiji went still.

"I mean, don't get any ideas or anything. I'm just asking. Besides, I figure it's a nonissue now that you know I'm—"

He put a finger over her lips, stemming the nervous flow of words. "When you are fully wolf, another wolf can imprint on you. That usually happens during sex."

She jerked her gaze to his, and he squeezed her arms.

"It is deliberate and not accidental in the heat of passion."

"Like a bite?"

"No."

"What then?"

"You open yourself mentally, physically, spiritually to me, and I to you. We bond and become as one."

"But Darryl…" A shudder passed through her. "Because he's my maker, he can force me to open up to him, can't he?"

"Yes."

She pulled from his arms and moved away. He let her go. "Can you do that to me?"

"No."

She squinted, trying to see deep into those dark eyes that grew pale when he changed. His wolf form seemed incongruent with his natural dark human looks. Still, it fit him too. Alone and aloof, a powerful animal that could unleash destruction yet chose to hold himself in control. Did he speak the truth? Could he force her just like Darryl? Maybe physically since he was a man. So many years she had depended on her strength and training, even on the people who had her back should she need them. In a short few weeks, two men had destroyed that illusion in their own way.

"Eiji, will you respect my decision, whatever it is, when I'm fully wolf?"

He watched her for a few long minutes, making her want to fidget, but she held her position as if his scrutiny meant nothing. "I will."

She strolled over to the hot tub and flipped a few buttons. The water churned, and soon she felt the heat. Colored lights lit the depths, and she pulled her panties off and let them fall to the terrace floor. Afterward, she raised her nightie over her head and tossed it away as well. She climbed into the hot tub and settled down.

Eiji stood at the side, so close. She hadn't heard him move, but the desire in his eyes radiated more than the water's temperature.

"Join me?"

He stripped. Shae bit her lip taking in the sight of his chiseled body, the contours of his chest and abs, the power in his thighs. His cock jutted out, hard and ready. She had visions of riding it until she grew exhausted and dizzy. He climbed in and settled on the opposite side of the huge tub. When he held out a hand to her, she didn't hesitate to take it and drift to him. Eiji sat on a ledge beneath the surface, and with strong hands, he lifted her to his lap.

"I was told not to touch you again," he murmured. She parted her lips to comment, but his covered hers in a searing kiss. His tongue delved deep into her mouth, and she moaned. She arched her back when his hands came up to her breasts, and he pinched her taut nipples.

"Mm, Eiji."

He caressed along her throat and nipped at her skin, too gentle to break the surface. He released one breast to explore between her legs. Slick with come, her folds parted as he drove two fingers inside. She whimpered his name once again.

"No one will keep you from me, except you. If you tell me no…"

"Don't be crazy. You're killing me, Eiji. I need your dick in me."

He started at her harsh language, but she grinned and turned to face him. His hold allowed her to spread her legs and rear up. Like they were meant to be together, his cock eased into her pussy, and her walls clenched, inviting him to go all the way. She sank with slow relish.

"Eiji." *I love you.*

She gasped, and his grip intensified. He jerked her close to his chest and thumped his cock hard inside her. The scream of pleasure and sweet ache echoed over the Hollywood Hills. Eiji's palms moved to her ass. He squeezed the two globes and thrust her forward. At the same time, he drove in. From gentle to rough in seconds, he pounded her poor pussy. She hung onto his shoulders, letting him take it all. Her thighs ached being forced so wide apart. Her pussy throbbed with its wonderful abuse. Eiji flattened her breasts and scraped her sensitive nipples over his chest, but with it her first orgasm rocketed throughout her body.

"Talk dirty to me, Eiji," she pleaded. "Tell me you're going to fuck me until I beg you to stop."

His eyes widened, but he didn't pause grinding into her.

"Say it."

"Shae." He covered her mouth and pushed his tongue between her lips. They sucked each other's and moaned as they greedily went after more. She came, shaking and moaning. He slowed just a little, but his cock remained hard. He pulled out and drove in at a more relaxed pace. When she leaned back, eyelids drooping, he teased a nipple with the tip of his tongue. Tingles of desire began to grow in her again. He moved to the other nipple and sucked it harder. The pain made her squeal in delight. He kissed along the curve until he reached the underside of her breast, then moved to the valley between them. All at once, he thrust hard and filled her to capacity. Her head spun. She thought she might faint, but held on, arms encircling his neck.

Eiji raised her up with hands at her waist and forced her down. She shouted into the night. He repeated the action over and over. She rimmed a second climax, but didn't fall over the edge. Her jaw grew slack. Even the ability to hold onto him lessened. All she had the strength to do was let him have his way.

He pulled out without warning, and she protested until he made her stand and flipped her around. She placed one knee on the shelf, and Eiji moved behind her and forced her to lean on the edge of the hot tub to keep her balance. He parted her ass cheeks and found his way down to her pussy. With a deliberate thrust, he drove in. A hand on either side of hers, he pounded hard and fast in and out. He kissed and nipped along her back, not missing a beat. And then his mouth was at her ear.

"I'm going to fuck you until you say it."

Pleasure rolled over her being. "S-Say what?"

"Say, please stop, *Goshujin-sama*."

Water splashed over the side of the hot tub as he took her with a violence and precision that satisfied them both. Eiji turned and sat down again, dragging her with him to his lap. His arms encircled her, and she rode his amazing cock until her hips ached and her thighs burned. She raised her chin to accept his kiss and welcomed his tongue as it twirled with hers. They moaned and moved in unison, and when she reached her umpteenth orgasm, Eiji reached his. The howl of the wolf filled the night, and she stared into his handsome face for long moments.

After some time, he helped her from the water and found towels for them to dry off. He took her hand, and they laced fingers together to move into the house.

"Are you going to leave me alone in my room?" she asked.

"I thought you might like to share my bed."

A chill raced over her skin, and all she could manage was a nod. They padded farther along the hall to the master bedroom, and Shae thrilled at the king-size bed. She climbed up, but before she could get very far, Eiji had crouched behind and kissed the backs of her thighs. He worked his way up to her ass cheeks and sucked the skin there. She keened in pleasure.

"Eiji, you shouldn't."

"You know how much I want it."

"I'm not telling you no." She climbed higher on the bed and turned over, raised her legs, and spread them so he could see her weeping pussy. "What does that word mean?"

"What word?"

"The one you said outside."

He seemed hesitant to tell her.

She played with her breasts and lifted one to lick her nipple.

A burst of air blew from his nostrils as if he had a hard time not attacking her. "*Goshujin-sama.* My master."

She laughed. "You've got balls. So you want me to say, 'Please stop, Master?'"

His fingers curled around her ankle, and he gave it a tug. He bent down and licked a tiny spot, which sent shivers along her legs, straight up to her apex. Her core muscles clenched. Eiji had a big appetite for sex, but the changes occurring in her increased hers as well. She could match him, no doubt. Could there be a greater synching between them when she was fully wolf?

Shae ran her fingertips across her breasts and down over her belly. She stopped at her pussy and then dipped one finger inside. Eiji's breath seemed to hitch in his chest. She caught her bottom lip between her teeth.

"I don't want you to stop, *Goshujin-sama.* I want you to make me scream."

Eiji didn't flinch at her butchering his language. The very fact that she'd tried appeared to send him over the edge. He landed on the bed and thrust her legs up higher. Her pussy gaped, and he ground his erection into her heat. She fell back against the pillows and shouted his name. He took her over and over, the friction and his weight above her driving her insane.

He yanked free and flipped her to her belly. Fingers buried in her wet pussy, then wet and entered her ass. She clenched her teeth together and arched her back. When he drove into her rear opening, she lost her breath. He lay across her body and eased deeper. Shae couldn't raise her head or open her eyes. Eiji laced his fingers with hers and seated his dick all the way to the hilt. She gasped.

"I can't," she panted.

He pulled all the way out and then drove in. Her head grew light. He murmured words in her ear, but she wasn't sure if they were English or Japanese. Their bodies drew apart and came together. He fit so snug she thought it too much, but she didn't want him to stop.

"Eiji, Eiji," she chanted.

"Tell me I'm the only man who can have you like this. Say it."

She moaned. He thrust deep and pounded against her ass. She struggled for breath. An orgasm came just close to cresting, and she buried her face in the pillow.

"Say it."

Shae turned her head and looked back at him. His eyes had gone pale, and white strands tinged his hair. Tingles of awareness zipped along her arms. An overwhelming ache to belong to him in every way imaginable came over her, until she couldn't bear to resist him. This wasn't like what Darryl had done to her. She didn't feel violated or swept along in a direction she didn't choose.

"You're the only one, Eiji. I'm yours."

He pulled her up and wrapped his arms around her, pinning hers to her chest. With their lengths sealed together, he continued to take her nonstop, and she dropped her head onto his shoulder, eyes shut, tears streaming down her cheeks. All she wanted was to give in to everything he demanded, to belong to him, heart, body, and soul.

Eiji thrust deep and held himself inside her. She gasped at the warmth spreading in her abdomen. He licked a tear from her cheek and touched his forehead to hers. They stayed in that position for a long while, and later stumbled to the bathroom to wash off the remnants of their lovemaking.

* * * *

Shae woke up and found the bed empty. Over the last few days, she hadn't ventured far from Eiji's arms. He made love to her several times a day, sometimes rough, but often gentle. He spoke to her words that were instructive and soothing. He never explained why, but she sensed he prepared her mind and the awakening wolf within her to accept the change when it came. Terror struck so hard she found it difficult to breathe, and then extreme peace, like nothing mattered except being with Eiji. All of it confused her, and she longed to run, to hide. Stubborn determination kept her from that plan, but it also kept her from fully accepting her fate too.

She tossed the sheet aside and stood, then padded to the bathroom. After a quick shower and brushing her teeth, she went to find Eiji. She found him on the terrace doing his morning exercise. Shae leaned against the doorframe watching him perform those fluid movements that she'd seen few others aside from his own nationality do so well. He raised both hands in front of his chest and pushed out while releasing a sharp breath. A half turn, and his leg shot out at lightning speed to kick an invisible opponent. She imagined whoever it was would be dead or have crushed bones.

Eiji wore *gi* pants and no jacket or shoes. She admired the way his muscles flexed and the light sheen to his skin from his workout. *Damn, he's sexy. How am I going to give him up?* A sharp pain struck her somewhere in her chest, and she chose to ignore it.

"Good morning," she called, and Eiji turned his head to glance her way. He didn't lower his leg, yet he kept complete, unwavering balance. Shae smirked. "Showing off?"

"*Ohayou.*"

She knew the word for "good morning" and didn't question him about it. "So what are we doing today? I mean other than fucking like bunnies."

He frowned, and she laughed. She enjoyed seeing the disapproval in his expression from her choice of words. Despite the look, she knew Eiji accepted her for the way she was. He didn't try to tell her how to speak. Although he had tried to teach her more Japanese over the last few days, which made her wonder if he harbored hopes she'd go back home with him.

"We need to work on you learning to center yourself more. We're running out of time."

She waved her hand. "The full moon is still two days away, and you said turning is the most natural thing in the world."

He moved to grab her hand and brought it to his lips. A tremor raced down her spine. His piercing eyes arrested her. "You pretend not to be afraid, Shae. I know you are scared. I'm not going to leave you."

She looked away. "You know what I am, or rather *who* I am."

"I can't change it."

"Change what?"

He raised her chin and kissed her lips, then entered the house. She followed. He'd used that cryptic way of speaking before, and it pissed her off. At first she thought he had just forgotten some words, and she also knew in the Japanese language, they used far fewer words to express themselves than English speakers, but Eiji meant something else. She was sure of it.

She grabbed his arm to pull him back, and desire licked her flesh at their contact. Her heart sped up. Lately, the feeling between them had intensified. "Explain it to me so I understand, Eiji!"

His gaze swept over her body, and her temperature rose. Her nipples pebbled, and moisture started between her legs. He sighed, but she saw the need in that dark gaze that could go so pale when they made love. She found she wanted it to happen now.

"I've marked you."

"What!"

He pushed hands through his hair and paced away. "I didn't mean to do it. It happened when you opened yourself to me while we were in bed. After I realized, I pulled back."

"But you said that can't happen until I'm fully wolf, and I have to want it!"

He looked at her. She dropped onto the couch and ducked her head. She had wanted it. She'd wanted to belong to him and nobody else. That's why she couldn't stand the thought of leaving him.

"We're not mates, are we?"

"No, we aren't. We can't until you change, but…"

"But what?"

"I expect Darryl to find us sometime today."

"What? Why?" Panic set in.

Eiji spoke in that infuriatingly calm voice that, at the moment, grated on her nerves. "He will have felt his connection to you weaken. He will know what it means, and he will come for you."

She sucked in a deep breath and blew it out. "Then we have to be ready. Do you have any weapons in this house?"

"Don't worry."

"Don't tell me not to worry. I *am* worried! I'm not letting him take me again, Eiji. You don't know what it's like to have someone in your head, controlling what you think and what you feel." She started searching through drawers and closets without his permission. "Besides that, he'll probably bring all his people, and you're fine as hell—you look awesome as a wolf—but you'll need backup, and I'm it."

He leaned on the back of the couch, arms folded over his chest, and a rare smile lighting his handsome face. "I like my odds."

She grinned. "You better, or I can kick your ass too."

Before he answered, she looked past him and spotted something over the mantel. "Cool, is that real?" She took down the sword and unsheathed it. The blade gleamed.

Eiji strolled up behind her and brought his arms around her. "This is a katana. Do you know how to handle it?"

"Swing and don't miss?"

He began instructing her, guiding the movements of her hands, the balance of her weight in her legs. Shae had handled knives, even short swords, but the katana was much longer. At first she found it awkward, but determination to remain free while helping Eiji made her work hard. She'd give anything to have her own weapons, left back at the house in her car, but she would make do.

"I don't like waiting. We should go find him."

Eiji shook his head. "On the chance he will wait until after you change, we need to stay here."

"I can stay calm."

"I don't want to risk you."

They stared at each other, and she thought she saw something warmer than concern in his gaze. If he had marked her, it meant he opened himself to her as much as she'd opened herself to him, didn't it? She dared not ask, especially since she still didn't know if it would lead anywhere.

"Eiji, you said I can't remain a rogue wolf. Why not? You are."

He removed the sword from her aching hands and re-sheathed it, but he didn't place it back on the mantel. The fact that he trusted her to use it said a lot, and she appreciated that.

"You have a little more protection because I've marked you. Any shifter you meet will pick it up and know you belong to me."

She glared at him.

"However, a single female wolf shifter is a lure for many different kinds of shifters, not just our kind." He seemed to think about how to make it clearer. "You are a sweet dessert that they will all want to taste and then possess."

She shook her head. "What, will they smell it on me?"

"Yes."

"Oh." She'd been kidding. No one had ever told her these kinds of details.

"Without a mate, wherever you go, you will have men coming after you trying to mate with you."

Shae clenched her hands at her sides. "By force?"

Eiji took a step toward her, but she stepped back.

"This is why my family—"

"It's their nature."

"You mean ours, don't you? The nature of rape?"

Something blazed in his eyes. "No, the nature to make you submit."

"Fuck that."

She marched into the bedroom and started going through her suitcase looking for something to wear. The clothing she'd worn over the last few days lay bundled together in preparation for repacking them.

"Shae, I don't make the rules."

"No, you just exploit them."

"I didn't force you." The clipped, biting tone angered her all the more.

"How do I know that?"

He snatched a blouse from her hands and tossed it on the floor. The next instant she found herself flush with the wall and him pressing so tight against her air couldn't squeeze between them. Shae's body lit on fire, and try as she might, she couldn't get the stupid thing to calm down.

Eiji breathed in deep through his nostrils. "You're telling me I'm making you feel what you feel now?"

"Get off me, Eiji."

He shifted his hips, bringing his hardening cock in contact with her belly. She bit off a moan. His torture continued with a nip at her bare shoulder. Her pussy throbbed.

"All the times you opened your legs, I made you do it? And when you said, 'Don't stop, *Goshujin-sama,*' that was me and not what you desired?"

She cursed him under her breath. "I said let me go."

He held her a little longer and then backed up. Shae went about packing her things, and when she went to lift her suitcase from the bed, he edged her aside and did it for her. She hated how she lusted after the bastard.

"Just...just sit it over there in the corner," she snapped.

He made no comment but did as she asked. For the rest of the day, they didn't talk much. Eiji cooked while Shae practiced with the katana. She refused to let him show her by touching, so he instructed with words alone, and at the end of the day, exhausted, she fell into bed. Eiji stood in the doorway, and she felt his eyes on her. She rolled over.

"Are you coming in?"

He strolled forward and kicked the door shut, and then lay down next to her. Shae wanted to keep arguing, to tell him he was wrong, but she settled into his embrace, and just like he said she would, she spread her legs for him to feel his shaft sink deep inside her heat. *Damn you, Eiji, for making me love you.*

Chapter Eleven

A noise woke Shae from her sleep, and she discovered whatever it was had awakened Eiji first. He stood at the door with his hand on the knob. He wore pajama bottoms and no shirt, and she rolled silently to her feet and slipped on a pair of shorts and dragged a T-shirt over her head. The katana lay on the carpeted floor beside the bed, and she caught it up and unsheathed it. She smelled them now, Darryl and his boys, and if the distinctive scent were any indication, they were already inside the house.

Glass shattered somewhere nearby, setting her teeth on edge. Eiji's broad shoulders shifted as he loosened his muscles, but before he could open the door, someone thrust it wide, sending him falling backward. Three men advanced into the room, one morphing into a wolf as he ran. The beast landed in the middle of Eiji's chest, but Eiji threw him against the wall. The crunch of bone gave Shae a sense of satisfaction, but she had no time to focus on her lover. More people flooded the room. From the look of it, Darryl commanded more than she'd thought, or he had allies.

Throwing caution to the wind, she sprang into action, swinging the sword just as Eiji had taught her to do. The sharp blade caught the end of a man's arm, and he made the mistake of trying to stop it with his bare hand. Blood spattered onto the carpet.

"Even a werewolf isn't invincible, fool," she sneered at him and went after the next bastard who came at her while the last crouched on the floor holding his wounded hand. A flick of her wrist and a lunge dragged the sword across the man's torso. He crashed to his knees, growling like a wolf, but it did no good with the amount of blood pouring from his wound. Shae kicked him in the chin to send him the rest of way to the floor. He didn't get up again.

Somehow she fought her way to the hall and then down it to the living room. The mistake came when she ran into the spot where someone had smashed a lamp. Shards of glass cut into her feet, and she lamented not taking the time to put on shoes. The momentary distraction was enough for someone to grab her from behind and wrap a muscled arm around her neck. She gasped for breath and kicked back at his leg. He winced, but his grip didn't lessen. The tighter he squeezed, the less strength she retained to hold onto the katana. The weapon clattered onto a nearby table and then rolled off to hit the floor. The next instant, Darryl appeared before her, and the man holding her let go. The back of Darryl's hand and his hard knuckles connected with her jaw. Despite locking her jaw, the blow wrenched a cry from her, and she slammed against the wall.

A growl of rage seemed to shake the house on the hill. Several men screamed in pain, and a small crowd of them fell backward from the hall. They didn't stay down long, but sprang up to their feet, Eiji stalking in wolf form. With the moon shimmering through the open terrace doors, his white hair shined like something ethereal. For a moment, they all appeared to be transfixed, and time stood still. Then Darryl came to his senses and grabbed Shae again by the throat. She struggled to get free to no avail.

"Stop," he snapped at Eiji, who had coiled to attack. "Before you can reach me, I'll have crushed her windpipe. I told you not to fucking touch her, but I can smell you all over her. You marked her, you son of a bitch. She's mine."

Eiji shifted and stood on two feet. The white hair receded, all except for the silken locks on his head. She couldn't help thinking how sexy this Asian man looked with pale hair, but it also told her Eiji was on the edge of a rampage.

"He killed Travon," one of the men told his alpha. "And John and JD."

"Kill *him*," Darryl roared.

Several men sprang forward.

Shae screamed, "No!"

"I challenge your position as alpha," Eiji blurted.

Everyone froze.

"Who the fuck you think you are challenging Darryl," one of the guys spat.

"He has the right."

Shae glanced at the man who'd spoken, and something told her he was close to Darryl. He seemed calmer than the others. When he had spoken, the man criticizing Eiji fell silent and stepped back a pace, but they all looked at Darryl. When he said nothing, Eiji cut in again.

"If you're afraid…"

Shae's knees gave out, and she sank to the floor finding herself released.

Darryl sucked his teeth and sneered at Eiji, eyeing him up and down. "Afraid of what? Give me room."

Everybody fell back, including Shae. Trying to keep her gaze on the two men circling each other, she dug bits of glass out of her foot. Her heart raced so hard it hurt. They fought over her, and she was tempted to yell she didn't want either one of them, but that wasn't true. She wanted Eiji, and she definitely didn't want him dead. Darryl beating him didn't bear thinking on. She searched her surroundings for the katana, not giving a damn about their rules. The minute she got a chance, she'd take the bastard down, but someone must have picked up the sword because she didn't see it.

A hand dropped on her shoulder, and she jumped. She peered over and found the guy she had studied earlier. When the hell had he crossed from the other side of the room to stand next to her?

"If your boyfriend wins," he whispered to her, "he gets to be alpha, but that won't last long, because I will challenge him."

Dread closed her throat. Did he have so little faith in Darryl? Did no one in his group really respect him? The latter wouldn't surprise her, and she prayed this guy was right in his guess about the outcome of the fight. Then again, Eiji would have to go up against him in order for them to get away, and he would be tired.

When Darryl sent Eiji over the back of the couch and into a glass table, Shae sprang forward. The man at her side gripped her arm, holding her in place.

"Get your damn hands off me." She threw a punch toward his face, but he caught her fist. He twisted her arm behind her back and dragged her to him from behind. Shae stomped his foot, causing him to suck in a sharp breath.

"Man, you're a bitch," he snapped. "I like my women easy."

"They'd have to be," was her quick comeback.

To her surprise, he laughed. "I'm not going to hurt you. Just let them do their thing. If you promise not to try to jump in it, I'll let you go."

"I'm going to do whatever I need to, to help Eiji."

He stared at her for a minute and then shook his head. "That idiot never had a chance."

She frowned at him. "What are you talking about?"

A shout of alarm went up, and they both turned back to the fight. Terror and pain rocked Shae's being when she saw the blood running down Eiji's arm, but then she transferred her gaze to Darryl. He lay on the floor unmoving. Even on the other side of the room, she saw that he wasn't breathing. The large brown wolf's body curled unnaturally, and as he lay there, he began to return to human form. Eiji had shifted as well and knelt on one knee holding his injured arm. His dark eyes scanned the room and rested on Shae, then the man who held her. Black bled to pale gray, and a snarl rose in his throat.

The man next to Shae let her go and grinned. "Now it's my turn. I'm second in line, and I'm going to wipe the floor with your ass. You don't belong here, and you definitely won't be our leader longer than it takes me to kill you." He stepped away from Shae. "I challenge you for the position of alpha."

"Can't you see he's been hurt?" Shae ran to Eiji and stood in front of him with her fists raised to the other shifter. If she had to fight on Eiji's behalf, she would. A protective instinct rose in her that she'd never felt before, and just as had happened on the beach, the metallic taste of blood filled her mouth. She'd begun to turn again, but she knew the risks. What mattered most was saving the man she loved. *Damn it all to hell, when did I get so soft?* "Come at me! I will be the one to fuck you up."

Eiji's good arm shot out from behind her and encircled her waist. "Shae, no."

"I say let her fight," someone called out with amusement in his tone.

More glass breaking distracted everyone from the pending fight, and then Shae and all the rest were coughing with burning lungs. Smoke filled the room, along with a pungent odor. Beyond it, she picked up an unmistakable scent—her brother's.

Pandemonium hit the house. Bullets flew through the air, and men shifted to their wolf forms in seconds.

Eiji tossed Shae to the floor and landed on top of her. She beat against his chest. "Stop, Eiji. Get off me. You have to get out of here, or they'll kill you. *Please!*"

He gazed with narrowed eyes at several points where they might escape, and she followed his line of vision. The windows, the doors, all were crowded with men flooding the room, guns drawn. "I'm not leaving you."

"Once my brother sees me, he'll make sure no one kills me, and I'm pretty sure none of the wolves will either. Right now, you're still alpha, and I'm...I'm yours."

He stared down at her. She saw a flicker of emotion in his pale gaze. As if in slow motion, he began to change. Her heart ached. He had to get out. She licked her lips, swallowing to try to wet her dry throat. Scanning the room, she searched for anything or anyone who could help Eiji. A bullet sliced through the air, and her lover jerked hard. An expression of pain crossed his features, and she screamed. Animal growls rose above human cries, and Shae realized they were her own. She stood, and Kasen appeared before her. *How did they find us?* Her brother's harsh glare bore into her, and then he cocked the gun in his hand and pulled the trigger without hesitation. Everything went black as Shae went down.

* * * *

"She's one of them. I say we kill her now and get it over with. After all, we're back on top. That new information specialist we hired is the shit. His idea of finding out if her rental agent owned any other properties in the area was brilliant."

That was Kasen, her heartless brother. Now she knew how they'd found her. Shiya had already been replaced, and it looked like nothing would stop her family from killing all shifters. Shae opened her eyes and scanned the room. She lay on a bed, handcuffed to the rails, in a bedroom she recognized as being at her father's house. No one appeared in her line of vision, so she assumed she'd heard the voices coming from the hall. An ache in her side caught her attention. She raised the dress she wore to find bandages on her side. Her bastard-ass brother had shot her. When she got her hands on him, she'd wring his neck.

"And I told you, son, I'm not ready to kill my baby girl in cold blood."

"Dad, you've always been too softhearted with them," Kasen railed. "You know there's no coming back from this shit. She's a werewolf, as far as we're concerned, the strongest and the most vicious of the shifters. Our mission is to—"

"Don't preach to me what my mission is, boy!"

Kasen fell silent.

Their discussion continued, but their voices faded, and Shae figured they had walked away. She breathed a sigh of relief. At least she had a little time, but what about Eiji? Had that shot killed him? Was he safe? She shut her eyes and breathed deep. Before she could figure out what to do, the door opened, and a woman entered. This was the lady her father was dating, a friend of the family for years and her mother's best friend.

"Gladys," Shae murmured and tried to swallow, her throat still dry. "Please, help me. I—"

"Don't." She crossed the room with a tray and set it down on the nightstand next to Shae. "You didn't follow procedure, Shae, and got yourself into this. I heard how that one protected you. You were lovers, weren't you?" Her disgust radiated.

"Where's Eiji?" Shae demanded. She rattled the handcuff.

"How long have I been asleep?"

Gladys picked up a needle from the tray and flicked it. Shae stilled.

"You are not using that on me. Gladys! When I get free, I'm going to—"

"What? Kill us all?"

The calmly spoken words were the strongest proof to why they had been doing what they'd been doing all this time. Shifters were violent. They had no qualms about killing humans, but Shae knew that was wrong. She did have qualms— and pain and loss. She lay in this bed in her father's home with her family around her, yet there couldn't be a wider chasm between them.

"You were only out since last night when your brother brought you in. It broke your father's heart to learn you'd been whoring with those things. Well, you're going back to sleep until he comes to his senses and has you put down."

"Don't do this!"

The needle pierced Shae's arm. She jerked away, and the bed frame bent. Gladys's eyes widened. She stumbled backward. Shae might not be able to break the metal cuffs, but the frame wasn't real metal. She tugged hard again, but her brain had already begun to fog over.

"No," she mumbled. "You have to let me go. Tonight …tonight is the…" *Full moon. I need an alpha. I need Eiji.* She hadn't the strength to say it out loud. Sleep claimed her once again.

* * * *

Shae opened her eyes to low light. The room had begun to darken, and the knowledge of what that meant scared the crap out of her. Already, she felt it inside, that stirring of something wild and inhuman. The beast strained to take control, and she knew her grip would slip.

"Eiji," she cried out in longing.

"*Hai.*"

She started and scanned the room. There he stood in the corner near the window. "You were here. You're alive." Her babbling grew worse as he approached, and her heart pounded. Her fingers ached to touch him. She needed to look him over to make sure he was okay. When he bent beside the bed, something clinked, and she realized he was using a lock pick on the cuffs.

"How do you know how to do that?"

He paused long enough to cast her an amused glance. Damn, she'd missed that handsome face, even if it had been merely a day since she'd seen him last.

"I was not always a policeman."

"Hm, I bet."

The cuffs fell away, and she launched herself into his arms. They both winced in pain, and she drew back, alarmed. "You were shot."

"So were you." Rage appeared in his gaze. "It is my right to kill them. You belong to me, and anyone who hurts you must die."

She grinned. "Thanks, baby, but now is not the time to go all caveman—or wolfy, I guess. Then again, it is. The full moon will be in the sky soon. Eiji, I don't mind admitting I'm scared."

He drew her close and raised her from the bed to set on her feet. The dress she wore did not include underwear, and she saw no shoes in the room. *Thanks a lot, Gladys!*

"I have taken care of you from the start, and I will continue. We will go somewhere safe."

"There's security. How did you even get in here?"

151

Eiji appeared affronted. She had visions of him doing some ninja moves on the guards, and would have laughed if the situation weren't serious, but what about the security system?

"As I said, I was not always a policeman, and even in my line of work, I have learned how to get around certain barriers."

She studied his handsome face. "Okay, I'll take your word for it."

He took her hand, features becoming set. "Stay close. You will be free soon."

In a short while, they were on the road, driving to who knew where. Shae clenched her jaw tight and crouched in her seat, at the same time taking peeks at the sky. On one hand, she willed the moon to come. On the other, she wished it would never appear. The dread knotting her stomach and making her feel like throwing up was the human side. The chomping at the bit, a sense of freedom coming soon, she knew had to be her wolf. Still, that wasn't all the beast felt. She also craved Eiji. She actually wanted to be his mate, strained in a way that had Shae wanting to raise her chin and expose her neck to him. What the hell did that mean? Another bite? Hell no. She would not give in. Every fiber of her being pleaded for it.

"We're almost there. Another five minutes," he informed her.

She bunched her hands into fists on her thighs. "Where are we going, and how do you know about the place?"

"Marcus told me about it. He set it up."

"Who?"

"He was Darryl's second."

Shae went cold. That guy had also challenged Eiji to be alpha of the pack now that Darryl was dead. "You shouldn't trust him, Eiji. He wants to kill you."

Eiji reached over and grabbed her hand. "Don't worry. He doesn't need to kill me anymore."

"What does that mean?"

"It means I gave him the position of alpha in exchange for helping me with you."

She stared at him in silence.

"The others will be here soon."

He turned onto a road that led deep into a wooded area. At the end of it, a small box home sat, nothing fancy, just serviceable. No vehicle stood outside, so she assumed the others hadn't arrived yet.

Eiji stopped the car and turned to her. He took her hand. "Shae, I will help you to change and make sure you are safe. What you want to do after that is your choice. I told you, you can't remain a rogue wolf. Men will try to take you, shifters of all kinds. The beast compels them to try to..." He searched for the word.

"Conquer me?"

"*Hai.*" His big, rough hand brushed her cheek, and her belly did somersaults. "I will stay with you and protect you."

Her eyes widened. "Wait, you're saying you'll go wherever I want to go and just protect me, not be my mate. Just be there? From what you're saying, you know how many fights you'd have to put up with? I mean, unless I stumble onto some place where there aren't any shifters."

He nodded.

"Eiji, why would you do that? Because you marked me? Look, I know it was an accident. It's fine. You don't have to throw your life away because of me. Hell, one life lost between us is enough." Feeling sorry for herself was not a part of her nature, but she wallowed in it for a few moments, her head lowered, while she dealt with the emotions.

"You don't understand." He raised her chin. "Shae, *aishiteru.*"

She opened her mouth to ask what he'd just said when a

ripping pain shot down her back. She screamed, but the pain didn't let up for a second. Muscles spasmed at every inch of her body, and bones seemed to melt with a fiery heat that made her gag and sob. Eiji pulled so hard at the seatbelt covering her chest, the fabric tore in two. He dragged her into his arms and kicked the driver-side door open. Metal ground against metal. Shae hardly noticed the door hanging at an odd angle as Eiji carried her up the steps to the house and shouldered his way inside. More pain blinded her, and spots danced before her eyes. Her head lolled on her neck, and she passed in and out of consciousness.

"Eiji." She screamed his name, or thought she did. Her voice came from so far away, and her lover's response didn't seem close by either. She cried harder thinking he'd left her, but someone squeezed her hand. The sensation pierced the pain ravaging her being, but not by much.

"Listen to my voice, Shae. Hear me," came Eiji's commanding tone.

His voice seemed to tug at her soul. From the darkness and pain, he was a beacon, and she followed, reaching out to him. Somewhere behind the blindness, a light shone. Eiji stood there, at first a man and then a beautiful white wolf.

He spoke, but she didn't see his mouth move. She heard his words in her head. Was this real, or had she fallen into a dream?

"*Shift, Shae.*"

"*I can't. It hurts.*"

"*You can. Let me help you.*"

Again, the pull, and a gentle, vibrant energy, surrounded her. Eiji's power eased her suffering. He invaded her mind, but not in a bad way. He chased the demons away and reached out. She took a tentative step forward—whether mentally or physically, she wasn't sure. He appeared closer, still sitting in the middle of a meadow. Weren't they in a house? The wolf raised his nose and howled to the sky, where the moon shone bright. The sound echoed through her head and heart, but then something inside her whined to do the same. She shrank back, ashamed.

"That's too weird. I can't do it."

He howled again, and her wolf croaked a small sound so pitiful she wished she could laugh.

"Shae, come here!"

She was all of a sudden in front of the white wolf, on her knees and naked. She put her hands up over her breasts. *"How did we get out here?"*

"The pain is gone, isn't it?"

She blinked at him, but he spoke the truth. She didn't hurt, and the confusion had cleared. Still, this place, she knew now they were in her mind together. They hadn't left the house. She felt the couch beneath her, which Eiji had laid her on.

The white wolf nudged her shoulder. She rubbed his head and scratched his ears. He whined, but when he stretched his nose to the moon the third time, she joined him. The sound that rose from her throat matched his, and the human melted away. In reality, she opened her eyes. She sat on the couch, her dress in a crumpled pile beneath her. Brown fur coated her body.

"Damn! I'm a wolf!"

"Hai."

She looked over to realize Eiji was in his wolf form too, and he'd just spoken in her mind.

"How?"

"I can't explain the mysteries of why we are the way we are. Do you want to run before they come?"

"They?" She remembered he'd said the pack would come and was surprised they hadn't arrived, but a sudden urge came over her at his words. *"Run."*

Eiji took off through the open door, and she bounded behind him. Outside in the dark of night, their paws ate up the ground. Shae's heart pounded, and her muscles grew warm. She dragged in deep breaths as she moved, and all of it felt so good she never wanted to stop. Eiji darted around trees and over fallen limbs. She matched every step, luxuriating in chasing him, in just being with him.

"Eiji."

She hadn't meant to make him stop, but he did, on a dime, and faced her. He padded over on silent paws to where she stood. His nose touched hers, and they nuzzled their faces together, unable to express themselves as humans would. She remembered the words he'd spoken in the car just before she started the change, but hesitated to ask him to translate. What if it didn't mean what she suspected it did? And what if it did?

"Eiji, I—"

"They're here."

He moved around her and fell into a jog. She had no choice but to follow. When they were close to the house, Eiji stopped running and blocked her path.

"Wait here."

He disappeared into the house and returned as a man wearing only pants. He carried her dress, and she breathed a sigh of relief as she shifted. "Whoa, I didn't even think of it. Or I did and just changed." Her words echoed loud over the quiet night.

Eiji smiled. "You will get used to it."

She dressed. "So they're here?"

"Yes. Are you ready?"

She pulled in a deep breath, blew it out, and then nodded. *"Hai."*

He smirked at her use of his language, and together they entered the house.

C hapter Shae stepped from the trees behind Eiji and noted the cars lining the drive. The others stretched out all over the living room, lounging as if they owned the place. Then again, maybe they did. Marcus sat in an armchair like the big dog on campus, with a woman perched on either side of him. He encircled their waists, hands low on their bellies, inches from their apexes. Shae tried not to gag and turned her head.

"So you got her here on time," Marcus said. "Good.. Have you decided what you're going to do?"

Shae glanced at Eiji. He nodded. "Thank you for the invitation to your pack."

"In other words, you're turning me down?"

While they spoke, Shae scanned the faces of the others. The women seemed less confrontational with her with Darryl gone, or was it because she was fully one of them? One or two of the men stared her down, unblinking. Their gazes shifted every now and then to Eiji, and she didn't miss the back-and-forth emotion between lust and caution. One of them moved as if to stand, but Eiji made a small noise in his throat. Marcus laughed, and so did one of the other men.

"Don't try, man," Marcus warned the guy. "He's marked her. I'm guessing he'll rip your throat out if you even try, and I'm not going to stop him. He's in his rights."

Shae's eyes widened. Were they serious?

"She's not his mate," was the snapped reply. "She's fair game."

"Fair game to fight for," Marcus corrected. He turned back to Eiji. "That reminds me. I wanted to say I'm sorry about your cousin."

Eiji's hands closed into fists at his sides, and a vein pulsed in his right temple. "Did he kill her?"

"Not like you think." Marcus sighed and sat straighter. He pushed the girls away, and they stood with reluctance. The man was going to enjoy being alpha too much. She hoped he'd make better decisions than the bastard who'd bit her. From what she saw, Marcus's head had already begun to swell. "She claimed to be a part of a pack where she came from. We are somewhat new in the area, so we didn't know for sure. Darryl didn't see a man around her, so he figured she was fair game. She said she'd fight him for the right to stay free."

Shae's mouth fell open. This was what Eiji had been telling her all along. A woman couldn't be a rogue, or she would find men coming at her constantly trying to make her submit. She ground her teeth in anger, and from the expression on Eiji's face, he didn't appreciate how Darryl had gone after her either.

"He accepted this?" Eiji asked.

"Yeah, he did. She wanted to fight him. He let her. He knew he would win, and when he had her down, she should have given up and let him take her."

"The hell she should!"

All eyes turned to Shae at her outburst. She folded her

arms over her chest and dared them to challenge her. No one seemed to care one way or another about what she thought, even the women. The two men who'd eyed her earlier still did.

"She pushed him until he hurt her too much. She could have recovered with his help, but Darryl didn't want to. He commanded us to stay out of it."

Shae hated every one of them. "And y'all obeyed, even with a woman dying right before your eyes." If she had the weapons now, she'd kill them without a second thought. "I don't care if I am a shifter. I'll never understand your ways. Ever!"

"There are methods to help you understand."

Marcus's mild reply sent shivers of dread racing up and down her back. She knew she couldn't stay in this area without protection. Either her family would find and kill her or these people would. She'd be reduced to fighting for her life just like Izumi. The sad thing was, the woman must have thought herself safe with no shifters in the area, at least none who wanted to dominate her. Then Darryl and his crew rolled into town. She wondered, with her training and her new ability to smell a person coming, would she have an edge? Could she go wherever she wanted? Maybe not without learning more about being what she was now.

Eiji cut across her thoughts. "I can't join your pack. I'm staying with Shae to protect her."

He'd said as much already, but hearing it again, seeing him admit before these men who viewed women as lesser than themselves that he wouldn't force her to be his mate, blew her mind. The women looked up at Eiji, and Shae thought she saw a flash of longing in their eyes before they masked it.

"She's got you whipped, man," one of the guys called out laughing.

"Thank you for your help. We are leaving." Eiji gave a slight bow. Anyone observing such a solid build, the stoic expression, and calm self-assurance would not classify Eiji as weak, and she loved him all the more.

No one barred him from taking her hand and leading her out of the house. They approached the car, and Shae climbed across the driver seat to the other side while Eiji tried repairing the damage he'd done earlier. She was tired, and she guessed he was too, but staying would be dangerous.

He settled behind the steering wheel. "Where do you want to go?"

She peered across at him. "Really?"

"I said I won't leave you, and I won't."

She chewed her lip. Admitting how she felt would take a huge leap of faith. "Let's go somewhere we can clean up and rest. Is that okay?"

"*Hai.*"

* * * *

Shae dropped the dress from her shoulders and let it slide down her frame until it crumpled on the floor in a soft pile. She stepped out of it and bent to fling the offending material onto a chair. She'd had enough of that dress and couldn't wait to shower and slip into the new things Eiji had bought.

While she stood in front of the mirror, he stepped up behind her, his hungry gaze on her breasts. A shimmer of a voice in her head whispered, *"Ours,"* but she couldn't determine if her inner wolf had said the words or Eiji's. Could they even speak into each other's minds anymore, or was that a skill only for her first change? Since the woods, she'd heard nothing of Eiji in her head, and for such a short-lived thing, her mind felt empty without him.

His hands settled at her waist, and a shiver of need sank from the center of her belly to between her legs. Her pussy moistened. Eiji's reflected image breathed deep, and his dark eyes paled. If she were even planning on telling him they would just be companions and nothing more on her journey to learning this new way of life, it wouldn't work.

Eiji ran his hand over the bandage on her side, and his eyebrows bunched. She knew he imagined killing Kasen, but since she'd shifted, her wound was nothing more than a flesh wound. Her ability to heal defied logic, but because it did, she believed Eiji when he told her he was fine. He wore a bandage on his thigh where the bullet hit him, but he didn't limp. Marcus and his people had cared for Eiji, and against their advice for him to stay still for a couple days, he'd insisted on coming to find Shae. She had to be grateful to them for that, and it said Marcus was at least a better man than Darryl.

"I'm okay," she told Eiji.

"I know."

"You said you were going to get my stuff in Venice."

He nodded. "I will."

"I want to go with you."

"No."

She turned in his arms and pressed her breasts against his chest. He hadn't yet taken his clothes off, and she intended to drag him into the shower with her. "I think I made that sound like a question. I meant, I'm going with you. We're not going to be apart from now on because…"

His gaze burned into her until she looked away. Her stomach muscles tightened. What if he'd changed his mind because of her being a Keith? He might be willing to look after her, but to be mated? No, she'd told herself this was it. She would admit her feelings.

She stared him in the face. "Because I love you, and I want to be your mate."

Bravado drained to her toes when he didn't speak.

"If you have a problem with that because of your family and all, I—"

He kissed her, hard and rough on the lips, and stuck his tongue into her mouth. His big hand engulfed her face as he nudged her chin higher. She lost the ability to breathe or think. He filled her heart, and her soul strained to belong to him.

When he raised his head, she teetered on tiptoe, but he held her close and stroked wetness from her cheeks she didn't know was there. "*Aishiteru* means 'I love you.'"

"Eiji," she breathed.

He kissed her then, and Shae forgot everything, all the fear, all the doubt, and the uncertain future. She knew nothing other than Eiji, and a certainty that being with him was where she was meant to be. She clung to him, arching her back so she snuggled into his body. They fit like they were made for each other, and when he drew away, releasing her lips, she rested her head on his shoulder with her eyes shut.

"We'll seal it," he murmured, and she looked up.

"I'm ready."

He didn't question her further. Maybe he was too afraid she'd change her mind. She stood before him watching as he shed his shirt and tossed it to the floor, then peeled the button open on his pants. Her mouth watered to see him in all his glory once again. His lean hips came into view, along with the light smattering of hair at his crotch. When his cock, hard and rigid, came into view, she longed to suck it. Every other time except the first time, he'd denied her, and even then he hadn't let her make him come.

Eiji took her hand, and they walked together into the

162

bathroom. The shower warmed quickly, filling the bathroom with steam. They stepped inside, and Shae thought she'd orgasm when Eiji began soaping her body. He ran slick hands down the outsides of her legs, only to come back up the inside. He teased her apex with flicking fingers across her clit. She fell against the wall and scarcely held herself upright.

"Let me wash you too," she offered. To her surprise, he handed over the shower gel. She squeezed the scented liquid into her palm, worked it into a lather, and then began exploring his body. Eiji's shoulders were tight with tension, but she kneaded the muscle and rubbed from his neck to his tight ass. "Damn, you've got a fine ass, baby."

He started when she smacked it, and she laughed. She stroked his thighs as he'd done her and ran greedy palms over his big cock. The tool twitched under her ministrations, and Eiji put his head back, allowing her control. She wanted to climb him like a monkey and ride him right there, but she held off. After a little while, Eiji made her focus on him.

"I'm going to bite you—small bite—and I want you to do the same to me. At the same time, open yourself. Let me in like when you changed before. Let us be one."

The process was simple and so easy. Once she'd determined she wanted to be his mate, she had no real qualms about opening her heart, and she felt him come in as if they bonded, two people becoming one. The steam rose around them, cocooning them from the outside world. Eiji held her so tight where he touched. She ached, and yet she wanted the same, to blend with him.

At first she'd thought mating meant giving up her independence to her man, to follow him without a choice. Now she knew it was so much more. Yes, she gave up herself, but so did Eiji. He would walk with her, and she would do the same for him. This bonding meant they could not—would not—subsist without each other. Now she knew, humans could never understand the level of commitment they shared.

"Eiji," she cried out.

"Shae."

He kissed her until her lips ached, and he pushed fingers between her legs to tease her bud. She whimpered his name out loud and in her head at the same time. He strummed her like an instrument, and she rose to her tiptoes, arching her back, clinging to his arms, as he brought her to a trembling orgasm.

When it ended and Shae's breathing settled, she kissed his shoulder and then dropped to her knees in front of him. His cock bobbed and bumped her cheek. She waited for him to say no and make her move, but he stared down at her—if she read it right—ready.

Shae licked the head and circled the cap. A shudder passed through him. The expression of bliss on his face took her by surprise. She stopped, but Eiji reached down and grasped her chin. He guided her mouth to his cock and pushed so that it parted her lips and eased inside.

"Suck it," he commanded, but not with unkindness in his tone.

Shae took as much as she could deep into her mouth, and partway down her throat, and then pulled back. Eiji hissed through his teeth. She pulled on his big, beautiful length with her mouth and lapped up his precome. Moaning against it set him off, and she smiled hearing him struggle for breath. For long minutes, she kept sucking, and then she worked him with her hand, pumping his length from base to tip. She used both her hand and mouth together, alternating that with teasing his balls. Eiji growled his pleasure.

"I'm going to come," he said, almost like an apology.

"I'll drink you, baby," she promised. "Let me taste it."

Eiji didn't hold back. He pumped into her mouth slow and easy. Whispered words escaped his lips, and then he found his release. She took every drop and sucked for more as she swallowed. When she was done, she licked his dick, letting it rest on her cheek, her lips, and even her nose. She kissed his thigh and stood. Eiji gazed at her, and she saw the love overflowing there.

"Why didn't you let me do it before?"

He squeezed off shower gel to begin washing her face. She didn't tell him she didn't use the stuff for her face, but then she had none of her toiletries. They would get them soon, right before they started their new life.

"You were not my mate before now," he answered.

Shae frowned. "Wait, so you were a virgin at getting head?"

Confusion colored his expression. She laughed.

"You've never had a woman go down on you?"

To her surprise, the look went from love to closed. He almost resembled the man she met that first day in Venice. "I won't discuss that."

"You're embarrassed?" she pushed. "Come on, Eiji. I'm not going to judge you. If you've never been with a woman—"

"I have!"

"Wow, the outrage." She stuck out her tongue, and he jerked her to him. Her heart thundered in her chest. Damn, she loved him. What would she do with herself, and what had she been thinking tying the knot that bound them so tightly?

Eiji pushed fingers into her short, damp curls and tugged light enough to sting but not hurt. An arrow of desire kicked her desires into high gear. "I have been with women. Not like you. I would not come in your mouth until I had given myself to you and to you alone."

Tears pricked her eyes, and she bit her bottom lip. "Did you know?"

"That you were my mate? From the first scent. What is the word? You intoxicated me, and I was lost."

She put her hands up and captured his face between them. "Eiji, *aishiteru.*"

He raised her into his arms, and Shae wrapped her legs around his waist. She clung to him, and they kissed, their tongues curled together. His fingertips grazed her anus, pressing lightly. She moaned into his mouth. Between them he started to grow hard again. She did her best to encourage it, rubbing against him, licking and sucking his bottom lip. When he lifted her higher to sink his erection deep into her pussy, she cried out in ecstasy. Her grip on his shoulders slipped, but it meant nothing at all. Eiji held her and drove her up and down on his hard-on with a speed and strength that boggled her mind. She whimpered and took everything he gave. He'd swollen so much, or her insides loved to cling to his rod. He stretched her walls and forced her legs wider the more he pounded her pussy.

"Eiji, oh damn, I can't...I can't take it."

He shifted their position so her back was against the cool wall. Still he thrust hard, pounding until her head spun. Her clit throbbed, and her core muscles wound tight. Waves of sensation threatened to throw her over the edge. She tried getting a grip, but with his onslaught, he made it impossible.

Sounds of the water streaming down on them, Eiji's guttural groans, and the slap of their flesh coming together took her to the point of no return. She came, screaming and pleading. Eiji never slowed his grinding into her heat. He wrapped an arm around her waist and drew her tighter. The new position scraped his pelvis over her clit. She wept on his shoulder, and a secondary orgasm rocketed through her being.

A long while later, after she'd gasped with a dry throat, and her heart began to settle, he let her legs down. They gave out, but he caught her and spun her to face the stream of water, him behind. Eiji sudsed his hands and rubbed them between her legs to massage her sore pussy. She let him do what he wanted because she had no energy.

When he finished, he cleaned himself and turned off the water. A thick towel wiped away all moisture, and Eiji carried her to the bed. She luxuriated in his arms, yawning.

"I want to take you here later," he said and touched her anus. She shivered.

"Mm, yes." She shut her eyes. "We shouldn't stay here long, Eiji. The sooner we're out of California, the better."

"I'll make arrangements. We will go to Tokyo."

"That'll be a nice change." Exhaustion began to descend. She didn't hear his reply, but drifted into a world of total sexual contentment, all at the hands of her perfect lover, Eiji. No one else would ever be needed besides him. That she knew more than anything else.

* * * *

Shae shifted in her seat on the plane. Her stomach hurt. Now that they were on the way, she feared meeting his family. He hadn't said whether he would tell them the truth, but surely they would figure it out by her last name. He'd said they would go to his hometown first and meet everyone. The honorable thing, he'd mentioned. Then she remembered he'd described himself as a rogue wolf, a loner. Eiji had separated himself from his family because in a way he was a misfit being a male wolf. If Eiji's family didn't accept her, that was just fine. She and Eiji would have each other's back, and that was all that mattered.

She needed to do one last thing before moving on with her new life. Since her cell phone had been destroyed in the mess at Eiji's house, she used a phone available on the plane and waited for the call to go through. Both excitement and dread passed over her at the voice of the person on the other end.

"Sakura, how've you been?"

"Shae." No one could instill more disgust in their tone than her oldest sister. "I've heard all kinds of stories about you lately. I'm assuming they're true?"

"If you're assuming, why ask?"

"I guess you're right."

Shae sighed and ran a hand over her face. She already regretted calling.

"Look, I know we haven't been close lately, but since I'm not going to be around…um…maybe for a long time, I thought you could follow up on something I was looking into."

Sakura laughed. "When have I ever been a team player, Shae? Don't be stupid."

"Get off your damn high horse and listen to me. Dad and Kasen haven't been too honest with us."

Sakura sucked her teeth, and Shae could just see her rolling her eyes. "Oh, what, now you're going to try to get me to turn my back on the family? You think we'll all get along? The Keiths are supposed to bow to the animals, is that it? You have no idea the storm that might come down on our heads, little sister. Fuck, what am I saying, there *is* a storm coming—because of *you*. But don't worry, we can handle it. You go on and hide with your new tail between your legs."

Shae swore under her breath. "Mom died in Miami, not Vegas. And it wasn't a bear that attacked her. Check into it if you want. Despite everything, I love you. Bye."

She slammed the phone into its cradle, knowing she'd done all she could. Eiji took her hand into his lap, and she leaned her head on his shoulder, preparing her mind for the trip that would take more than seventeen hours. And then…her new life as a wolf shifter.

The End

About the Author

Tressie Lockwood has always loved books, and she enjoys writing about heroines who are overcoming the trials of life. She writes straight from her heart, reaching out to those who find it hard to be themselves completely no matter what anyone else thinks. She hopes her readers enjoy her short stories. Visit Tressie on the Web at www.tressielockwood.com.

www.ingramcontent.com/pod-product-compliance
Lightning Source LLC
Chambersburg PA
CBHW022123170626
46808CB00002B/822